Goodbye

Bolinas

we'll see you again

By
Rainer Neumann

landseandsky

1

Published by

landseandsky

Cover art is a pastel drawing of an old VW relic overgrown with nasturtiums somewhere in Bolinas. This image is superimposed on a photo of an anonymous tie-dyed T-shirt. The typeface of the titles is Baka Too. The text font is Chicago.

This book is available through Lulu.com.

For further inquiries contact: highwayone@earthlink.net.

ISBN: 978-0-6151-3951-7

Dedication

To the friends who have left
And those who still remember

Goodbye

Bolinas

we'll see you again

Prelude

At evening's end we were sitting around the supper table when Barbara announced that Ellyn would tell us all a ghost story. In the process of cleaning and clearing the table Ellyn acknowledged the request with a quick retort, "I don't know any ghost stories."
But Barbara was not so easily dissuaded and replied, " Yes you do, the one you mentioned some time ago, remember, when you went north, along the California coast..."
"That's not a ghost story, that was a trip, it was real...it was..."
Barbara finished the sentence for her, "a ghost story. You never found her again, did you?"
"Not yet, or, let's put it this way, not the way any of us expected, but, you know, it wasn't just about her, you really have to go back to that summer in the sixties, it was a happening, it was an odyssey, a mindexpanding odyssey..."
"Well, c'mon then, it's a perfect story for the ending of the day. In this old farmhouse in Vermont, we need something to remind us of the West Coast, when it was an uncharted land, at least in its possibilities..."

Disillusioned and disheartened
Well, you think the world has forgotten
What you tried to do
When you wore your heart
For all to see
Hey hey hey
For all to see

8

1

I Was Just Out of High School

"God, it seems so long ago, I was, I was just out of high school, hitchhiking, if you can imagine, me, putting out my thumb on Highway One, jeez, in those days, what was I thinking, in those days you could do that, or you just did it, and I wasn't the only one, I had already met people on the road, in fact, I had met this straight-laced woman, who was a little older than me, I wondered what she was doing there, I do remember though, she had just left her husband, a molecular biologist, and here she was, studying psychology, a teaching intern at Stanford, here, standing on this mountain highway. She had just walked up from Mill Valley to the top of the ridge where you could look over into Muir Woods - Muir Woods - John Muir - Jesus, the man himself honored with a grove of redwood trees. I was just walking along the highway when I stopped fairly close to her. She was so intent on looking into the west, into that valley, into that grove, that she didn't even hear me when I asked her how she liked the view. It was only after some time that the spell broke and she noticed me. When I said, *great view*, she nodded, and I continued, *that's the John Muir grove of redwoods down there.*"

"I know," she said, "that's why I came up here. I've been there and I wanted to see it again from above because I've been in it, I've been surrounded by those giants, actually, immersed is a better word, like my life up till now..."

I was giving her all my attention as she bared her frustrated feelings, "I've been immersed in a marriage and an on-going academic treadmill, trying to understand human motivation by studying rats or trying to understand Maslow's level of needs, which has some validity, but I think he missed one, that is, he missed the need to let go! That has to happen after you fulfill those survival needs. I mean, how could you add something if there's no room to..."

"Slowdown," I said, "whoa..." I tried to stem her torrent of words, but she just kept on spewing them out. I thought I was the only one who could rattle on like that.

"How can you?" she said again, "how can anyone take on something new when the cup is full."

"Sure," I said, "Well, maybe you have to spill some or drink some..."

She looked at me with a quizzical smile and repeated, "Yes, you have to spill some and that's what I've done. From here, from this ridge, overlooking this valley, even those giants look small. I can take them all in, I can take in the whole valley, and I can go over this mountain, all the way out to the Pacific."

"And who knows where that goes," I said to her, until she grinned and came over to me.

"I think I like you," she said and put her arm around me and pulled me close to her and asked me what I was doing up here and when I got a little distance between us, I told her I was heading north, not exactly sure how far north, taking Highway One, you know, that fabled highway, like the song, *travelin on Highway One feeling the warmth of the sunuhuhunnn no matter where you've been no matter what you've done you'll feel like you have just begun...travelin on Highway One travelin on Highway One...*I'm going over Mt. Tam.

"Mt. Tam?" she repeated.

Yea, I said and continued singing, *found a way the other day to leave the crowds behind, such crazy ways oh noooooooooooo just let yourself gooooooooo travelin on Highway One...*Yea, Mount, and this time I used her beautiful whole name, Tamalpais, the sleeping maiden of Indian lore, Miwok lore, I'm going to walk, me walk, on her gently, that is softly, I don't want to disturb her, but I love her beauty, her soft beauty..."

"You sound like a poet," she said to me.

"You sound like a poet." I can still remember her saying that...coming from a Stanford psychologist. Can you imagine? She had definitely already spilled some of her life and her cup had some room in it and so it turned out we decided to travel together. In those days you could do that, just decide to travel together. She told me her name was Julia; that this sojourn of hers was like reading Herrmann Hesse's *Magister Ludi* and jumping into an ice-cold Alpine Lake. She said she was feeling so alive

10

with possibility, a kind of unknown possibility, that she was bursting with it. She was just, like so many of us at that time, just *bursting with it.* We stood there and we talked and we finally sat down and talked and occasionally one of us put up a thumb until some car honked and we looked around. On one of those occasions a VW van had stopped with a few stickers on it. I remember the back bumper, it had *Live Free or Die* on it or was it *Live Free and Tie-Dye*? Actually, it was probably the former and we argued over the State that motto came from. I said it was from Vermont and she, of course, was also a history buff and could name the original 13 states as well as recognize their mottos and she told me that that motto was from New Hampshire.

I said, "Neat, but what happened?"

"What do you mean? " she questioned, "What happened? What happened to them?

"What happened to that attitude? I mean, Jesus, that was 200 years ago and it sounds like something that just came out of Berkeley..."

"You've got a few things to learn," she said, and I remember just looking at her when the van honked again. We walked up to the door, looked in and saw this lean, bearded, longhaired guy behind the wheel.

"And where ya going? " he said, with a voice that sounded like the wind. Well...I exaggerate a little bit, but God, he just drew me in and I took her hand and pulled until we were both in the van which happened to have aqua blue sheepskin covers everywhere and before he could tell us where he was going, I just said, *"groovy..."* and my big sister - we were now sisters of the road - just kind of eyed him and looked around, she wasn't sure, but I, Jesus, I could feel his vibes. This guy was cool.

"Geez, it looks like a swimming pool in here." I told him.

He smiled and nodded and I asked him where he was heading?"

"I'm heading north, along Highway One, for a short ways, probably stopping in on one of the towns."

"Sounds good to me, " my sister said, having made herself comfortable in the sheepskin swimming pool.

"What's your name?" He was looking at me and I said, "well," and I just blurted out, *Bobby McGee* and he started singing, *busted flat on a mountain road, heading for the coast, feeling nearly faded as your jeans.* I joined in and we ended up singing every word of that Christopherson song, even attempting every wild croak of Joplin's finish until that VW rolled with rhythm around the curves of Mt. Tam and through the dappled afternoon sunlight.

"Sweet aloha," he suddenly said, taking a quick glance over at me, "Sweet, sweet, sweet, that's what I'm going to call you."

Geez, that just sent me reeling. I wanted to crawl all over him but I held off and he just kept on driving, both hands on the wheel until we were hugging the hillside, maneuvering around the corner of a deep ravine cut by a seasonal stream, around a hairpin turn, back out, overlooking a forested canopy of pines and moss covered oaks until the road opened up to the soft golden curves of the Princess and the expansive sky.

11

There, in between the sky and the land, was the great Pacific, named for its passivity, its peacefulness, yet, even from here, I could see it moving with constant surf and white-combed breakers. I was wide-eyed at such an opening of beauty. It was like I was seeing it for the first time. Even now the expansive setting reminds me of a monumental Bierstadt painting of the American west or an Adams photograph with colossal clouds or some idyllic movie backdrop, only it was real. Our smooth-tongued guide suddenly pulled over and let us take in the scene and without asking turned around and drove back up into the Pan Toll parking lot, Shiva, as he called himself, parked the van and asked us to follow him, while he played a penny whistle, along a narrow path into a ravine of rushing water darkened by redwoods. With ferns growing in the shadows the smell was a rich deep musty musky aroma of growth and layers of transcendent earth. The sound of trickling, flowing, occasionally gushing water accompanied us as we wandered our way down, through a steeper ravine, over rocks, even down a ladder built to accommodate those who couldn't find footholds. We continued down, past a gathering of large boulders, until the path leveled out and slightly ascended into another opening of golden grass and sky. We clamored up until the glistening sparkling ocean could be seen again and we all fell down onto the softness of the Princess' languishing body...just to be there...just to lie there...just to feel her breathing...

I fell into a timeless sleep and remembered waking to Julia's exhortations. She was standing feet apart, she had definitely opened up, her arms were reaching for the sky, reaching for the clouds, her voice resonating over the waves of grass which were becoming inundated with a rolling swiftly blowing cloudy mist. I can still see her standing in the midst of that cooling fog, that roilingtoiling cool air pulled from the ocean into the vacuum left by the hot inbreathing of the Princess. She stood there, her incantations resounded over us...*I...I am the eagle that flies...* where that came from I don't know but her hands and arms were stretching into the open sky...*I am the whale that dives...*her feet and toes were digging down into the ground maybe further...*I am the breath of life...*I could see her breasts heaving in and out with each gasp of the moist air...*I am the earth reborn...*her physical body seemed alive with the living growing earth around us under us in us...*I am the earth reborn*, she repeated over and over, each time a little quieter and deeper. Somehow her incantations moved me, I was caught up in her strange mental state, the swirlingwhirling of the surrounding rainbow colors, this wild spectrum of light was intensifying everything, until the ethereal mist enclosed us all...obscuring our outlines and our reason...it was some other time...some other time...

At some point I was aware of a cacophonous cawing and saw crows clamoring around us and, again, heard the gasping sounds of Julia. She was still buried in the psychedelic ground. She was still lifting her arms, moving and waving, to the soaring sky. I followed her hands high, only to go beyond the crows to see turkey vultures floating high on the soft hot

12

air, gliding over us, their shadows, occasionally, momentarily, eclipsing us. A random coincidence and yet, I felt, they could be an eerie omen or an intimation of things to come - turkey vultures circling - who knows what they were thinking or what they portended to be, even metaphorically – met a phor i cal ly – yes, they could just be manifesting a life of their own, or they could be, that is, they...my thoughts were outrunning me...

It was then that I noticed this tall presence next to me. Shiva, our cool guide, seemed to know what I was thinking while I was looking up at those windborne gliders. Somehow he put my thoughts into words, "We make these extensions of ourselves into something beyond ourselves. In this case a relationship between the lives of vultures and our three lives on the ridge of this golden grass."

And I thought, yeah, a concurrence on the falling skirt of the mountain princess. And then I thought, she too, this mountain princess, was a metaphor, she was my romantic projection onto a rolling coastal hill. Interrupting my thoughts, he continued to speak, this time with questions, "What is our life without our minds extensions and realms of meaning, or is our life just an extension of our habits? Are we so desperate to live; so desperate to continue the familiarity of our habits that we build walls of security around them? Is it only when natural disasters, man-made disasters and ultimately personal disasters strike, that we are shaken out of our habits of familiarity? I've been struggling with these questions and I've had to ask myself...*how can we shake ourselves out of our familiar habits and lives*?"

As his words flew into the mist, I turned my gaze onto his face. His eyes had closed, his body was gently rocking, he seemed to be on the verge of something...until he slowly opened his eyes, squinting, as if wakening to a bright light, his voice oozing forth...*ohhhahheeee*...his eyes glistening like moist fog on the blades of the surrounding grass, where petals of orangeyellow California poppies were opening up around us... *ahhhheeeeeeeiiii*...the sounds of each vowel were wavering in the air...he sang to us, he sang to the waking world of our senses... *ahhlaayluuyaaaaah*...his arms were moving in circles, I followed him, opening my arms, round, in forever circles...*ahhlaayluuuuyaaaaah*...our voices joined this mantra of the afternoon, this sound filling the hillside, moving like the mist, the flowing whirling mist, with our arms reaching, ever expanding and closing, expanding and closing over our hearts...

I remember this blurring of reality, as if it were in this room, I remember looking around, looking for Julia, she was here she was chanting she was no longer here, I gazed outward, only to find her floating over the misty robes of the princess, floating in the leftover *hallelujaaaaaah*, floating ever closer to the edge of the world, the sound of the surf breaking through the stillness...I can still hear it, still...*What was she doing? So close!* I thought, "SO CLOSE!" I finally yelled, but my voice was lost in the crashing surf, lost to her. "Too close! " I said again, "Too close..."

13

Before I could say any more, I realized Shiva was standing next to me. He had also witnessed her floating, fading, sinking presence...He was the first to shatter the stillness, by speaking, slowly, as if from a distance: "Throughout our history, many people have believed in self-sacrifice, in order to continue living."

"What are you talking about?" I spoke in a barely audible, incredulous voice.

"To die for one's belief or to die a hero or to die because we've gone into a state of ecstasy and want it to continue...somewhere...to continue... because in that moment we believe we can transcend mortality...

"Shiva, you're talking beyond me, did you just see what I just saw?"

"Are these just delusions of immortality? Somehow, somewhere, sometime, we human beings became aware of our mortality, our inevitable death.

"Shiva, what happened to Julia?"

His voice seemed alien to the ephemeral atmosphere, his words were from some other place, breaking through the mist, dissolving it, pulling it down, like a crazed destroyer of a made up world...was he, was he obscuring or clarifying the moment with his ideas? I held my breath, my head was swimming, I wasn't sure what was going on...

"Wha," I gasped, "what happened? "

"I, I'm not sure, I..." he stammered, as if waking from a surreal stream of consciousness.

"Let's go, let's go back up the mountain." I pleaded for him to come. We turned and never looked back, letting the redwoods devour us, swallow us, until we wound our way back up the mountain, until that parking lot opened up a large enough space for us to breathe. In silence we entered the van. I let him drive, let him follow the curved two-lane highway down the mountain, turning without thinking, in and out of the mountain pleats, hugging the side until the road opened to the wide vista of waving grass and the bay that held Stinson Beach. I saw it but I could not speak, my voice was still caught up in that strange dream, my mind wavering with what had happened; my mind   wanderingwondering - *Did it happen? I know she was on that mountain...why did we*...As he turned onto the coast highway, I tried to bury my questions in the mists of that mountain...leave them there...In silence he continued to drive into that beach town, through it, further...Along the water's edge, my hazy vision changed as sunlit white egrets poked their heads into the water. I could see a blue heron swooping low and rising again. Shiva drove that van around the perimeter of that lagoon until we crossed Mesa Road, turned left and came into a town, a hamlet with no name.

2

Mariah

He stopped in front of a cafe that had Scowleys roughly written over the door.
"Let's get some coffee," he said, as we walked in. The floor creaked. We sat at a counter with the worn remains of a history of names once deeply carved into its redwood grain, echoing a past and bringing them into the present - Red Ryder, Wild Bill, Donovan, Lucky Lucy, Highway One revisited...
"Hey, here's one that looks familiar."
"Let's see."
With his finger he follow the carved lines: K...E...R...O...U...A...C...
"Not theeee Kerouac?"
"You're damned right!" came a response from behind the counter. I looked up to see a bar towel, a dirty grease-stained apron, a deep cleavage and a blond-haired, wide-eyed woman bending over.
"Lemme tell ya, the day he put that signature into the counter he just had a poetry reading at the Community Center, he was there with some guy named Corso and they had just come in, followed by an entourage of devotees, including some women who had taken issues with their

15

buddybuddy personas. I can still see them..."

"Hey, just, when do boys grow out of being boys?" one of the women, oozing sarcasm, asked loud enough to stop the duo and demand a response.

"When they die, woman, when they die." Corso answered out of nowhere, grabbing his throat and falling onto the floor writhing in an agony of death, "Ahhrrrg..."

"This boy is in pain." Kerouac said, as he picked up a fork in the counter. "We must take this boy out of his misery." He held up the fork in a sacrificial gesture.

"No ooooo, please, I'll stop. Don't stab me no ooo..." It was so sudden and, for some, unexpected, that the room began to fill, first with a snicker, and then, finally, with out and out laughter.

"Yes," she said, "I was there, I must admit. I laughed at their histrionics, and the wild abandon of it...*God, we live such restrained lives*...After that I asked him, actually both of them, to carve their names in the counter."

She stood in her momentary silence, as if she was thinking about that chaotic moment, while we waited, looking at the wooden signatures.

"You see Corso's here," she finally said, pointing to a large 'S" with the letters O R S and O in it's, almost, circle. "Oh, I'll tell ya, that was a night."

"Anybody else?" `

"Are you kidding? Sure, take a look. Here's Russell's, He's a local hobbit, who comes in now and then and stays in a cabin the size of an outhouse on the Mesa. He started the poetry film group, you know, bringing some visual aesthetic to the literati – and some of them could use it..." She was moving down the counter now and my eyes were following her fingers outlining the carvings and scratches of what looked like 100 years of egotistical activity. "Here's one you'll know. Can you read it? It's almost worn off."

I looked closely and tried to follow the slight indentations...J L O N D O N.

"Jack London." my eyes widened.

"Before my time, but he was here...wrote some great stories."

"Wow, that's a while ago."

"Well, its...hold on, let me take care of the gatecrasher...Hollywood, I thought I told you to stay out of here until you get that table fixed."

"Yea, well, I just need a..."

"You're not gonna get nothing until the table is fixed. The one in the corner, the one you sat on, remember..."

I looked over to see a geometric serape on a wide grinning American Indian, his face a road map of character lines, with eyes that seemed to take us all in at once.

"I'm aiming to do it but somebody's taken my hammer, my whole tool box...and, as my grandfather used to say a tool is an extension of the hand.

"You've always got some excuse, Hollywood."

16

"Yea, but I could fix it if I had some tools."

"So, I have to bring you a hammer."

"Well, just let me borrow it."

They kept at it until she gave in, went to the back, brought back a toolbox and handed it to him. "Let's see what you could do with this. Just make sure I get em back."

"Mariah, you know I wouldn't take these." He half-jokingly stuck a hammer under his serape and headed for the door. When he got no response he turned and ended up at the remains of the table in the corner. Mariah just shook her head. "That's Hollywood," she said, looking at us. We smiled and settled down at the counter.

"Your name is Mariah?"

"Yep, they call me Mariah, because I came into Bolinas on one of those crazy windy days; the waves were breaking on the cliffs it was so windy. Somebody looked at me and asked me if I brought the wind and I just started singing, *Mariah blows the clouds around and sets the mountains crying Mariah makes the mountains sound like folks was up there dying...*"

"All right, Mariah, we hear you." Hollywood interrupted.

"I remember Josh, who works next door, saying, 'Mariah, that's gotta be your name, baby.'"

"Well, it stuck and I'm still bringing the clouds around..."

"Come on, you've made the afternoon..." she cut me off and asked, "So what are you two doing in this *Lost World*?"

"Well, we're not entirely sure but I guess we'll spend the night," Shiva said. "You think we can park our van somewhere?"

"Turn left at the corner towards the beach. Anywhere along there."

"That's great, and, now that that's out of the way, how about something to eat? Are you still serving?"

"Well, we usually close at three unless there's something happening, but I could get you a sandwich or some of my black bean soup."

"Black bean soup. Sounds great."

"We put a little something special in it."

She let them settle at the counter, gave them some water and a spoon and went to the back of the kitchen.

"Let me offer my services." The Indian made his presence known. "If you're on the road, this is a good stopping point. As my grandfather used to say, 'feel the earth as you walk and you will know when to stop'."

"That's a little hard in the van."

"Sweet, I think he means 'feel the vibes'."

"Are you a local?" Sweet shot back.

"Somewhat, my ancestors were Miwok." He answered with a quick quixotic smile.

"I would say you are historically local."

"Yes, to be sure, some would say hysterically local."

"So, why do they call you Hollywood?"

"Well, you are talking to the bane of Kemo Sabe."

17

"The bane? Who?"

"Not 'who' but 'how' as in 'how'. He raised his right arm and repeated 'how'. I was one of the articulate Indians on the Lone Ranger show."

"Not Tonto?"

"No, I was in the tribal cast of many. Maybe, you saw me with Cochise. That was probably my best part. I had to fall off a Pinto and bite the dust."

"The car?"

"The four-legged kind."

"So, you're a star?"

"I'm waiting for a call."

"How long have you been waiting?"

"Oh, a couple of years now. But as my grandfather said, 'It is not the time but the result that matters.' "

Mariah came back with two bowls. "Well, you're in luck, I still have some. It just happens to be the house specialty, I must add. Enjoy."

I didn't realize how hungry I was until I spooned that soup into my mouth. It was the best soup I had tasted in years, if you like black beans, that is, but this had a taste of…she finally said, sherry, in it. Wow, I can still taste it. And the funny thing is, that is, I found out some years later that this great soup came out of a Campbell's soup can and she just added a touch of sherry. But then I remember sitting there; it was like a warm fog coming over me; only it started inside. It was like being at my grannies when I was, before I was, before...before things changed, OK! I can still remember feeling that good. It was at my grannies. She used to make cream of wheat, or oatmeal or something like that, and I, she let me put brown sugar on it and marmalade and cream and I felt so warm, I wanted it to last forever." Her eyes closed and she disappeared...

Why can't I stay with granny? Please? I wanna stay with granny...I was grabbed by the wrist and pulled hard, almost coming out of my shoes.

"Damn brat, always wanting something else. Let's go. I've got to get you home."

"I don't wanna go home," I cried.

"Goddammit, I'm tired. I don't have time for tantrums."

It was no use. I was dragged back to mom. I didn't want to go there because they were always fighting. My mom acted strange. Ronnie would find a bottle hidden behind the couch and he would throw it and then my mom would jump at him and they would roll round on the floor until she told me to leave the room and clean up the glass. I had to. Sometimes I cut myself. Sometimes I closed the door and I heard them fighting on the floor. My mom would Scream and he would Scream and...after that, after a long time, she would call me and tell me how sorry she was and sometimes Ronnie was naked and grabbed a pillow to cover himself.

"Hey, where are you, Sweet face?"

Shiva's voice broke into this momentary lapse..."I don't want to remember," I winced, as he put his hands on my shoulders and looked at me, his eyes questioning...I shook my head and looked around the room - huge East Indian batiks hung from the ceiling like clouds with ornamental designs. Every kind of recycled chair and table was randomly strewn across the room. Now and then a jukebox would light up and randomly play an excerpt out of the past, *whatever will be will be, the future's not ours to see, what will be*...Silence again. There was a short somewhere.

"Is there something wrong with the jukebox?" I asked.

"It works on my command," Hollywood interrupted and walked around with his arms in the air, like a conductor beginning Beethoven's 5th. He let his arms drop and the sound of an old crooner began, *strangers in the night, exchanging glances...*

"Wow, you're a conjurer," I exclaimed.

"Yes, that I am, and that's not all." He came over to me, put his fingers behind my ear pulled out a pendant, a round peace sign.

"Peace."

"How."

"I'm not sure."

"Let's try it again."

"How."

"Peace." We all held up our fingers in the peace sign and let out spasms of laughter which continued until the Scowleys sign fell down and the jukebox came on with, *if you're going to San Francisco, be sure to wear some flowers in your hair...*

"Hollywood, you're a character."

"Yes, but I wanted to be a star, you know, with my name in the sidewalk, in front of Grauman's Chinese Theater. I mean, how many Indians have to die before one of us gets recognized. I mean, remember Wagon Train and Long Rifle and Little Big Man and..."

"O.K., O.K., we've got the message, you deserve it."

Mariah finally broke up the powwow and reminded us that she was closing, "Morning comes early for me," she said, "I serve breakfast here."

"Yes, well, we're going, thanks, we'll see you tomorrow, I hope." We shuffled out, and Hollywood gave us a piece of driftwood with his name carved in it as well as telling us his address – *Bolinas on the beach.*

"Thanks."

"That's where you can get a hold of me," he said at the entrance, "My hogan is on the beach, you'll find it."

We made it back to the van and, finally, crashed into the twilight.

3

Roderick

"Hey, anybody home!" a strident voice broke the stillness of the night, along with banging on the driver's door, "Wake up."
"Huh, I, who is it?"
"It's the sheriff, anyone in there?"
"It's the cops," Shiva whispered to Sweet and answered the sheriff. "What's the problem?"
"You're the problem, open up."
Shiva crawled over the front seat and rolled down the window.
"You can't park here."
"Why not?"
"What do you mean, why not? Because I said so, you long-haired beauty queen."
"Shiva, what's wrong?"
"He wants us to move..."
"Open up and come on out."
Shiva put his shirt on, "They said we could park here."

Sweet climbed over and looked out the window.

"Well now, how old are you youngster?"

"Eighteen."

"Yea, let's see some ID."

"I don't have any. It was stolen."

"You better come up with something or I'll take you both in."

"Look officer, I gave her a ride and we just want to sleep here. Just for the night. We'll be gone in the morning."

"She's a runaway, Longhair, and you could be in big trouble. I'll bet you've got some weed in there too."

Sweet couldn't hold her tears back. She burst out, "I'm not running away, I've got no home…this is my home…"

"All right, Long-hair, outta the van." He put his arm inside the window and opened the door. Almost instantaneously he used his right arm to pull Shiva's hair and dragged him out.

Shiva did not fight back but stood up and told the cop to hit him, that he was a nonviolent person, that he would turn the other cheek, which he did, and the cop was momentarily taken back, not sure what to do. Finally, he handcuffed one hand to the door handle.

"C'mon outta there."

"We're innocent." Shiva said in a tone that was both authoritative and an appeal to the man's sense of empathy.

"Well, let's see how innocent you are. Come on out," he said to the face in the darkness of the van."

Sweet finally emerged.

"Well now, just how old are you?"

"I'm gonna be eighteen."

"And that's what you call innocent, eh Mister."

"He's my boyfriend and soul mate."

"Oh he is, eh. Well, soul mate doesn't cut it around here."

"Officer, we are traveling and stopped here for the night. Isn't it better to get some sleep rather than fall asleep at the wheel?"

Roderick's eyes widened and he slowed down. You could see he was thinking about us. "I'll tell you what. Maybe we could make a trade. You let me have some of the weed you have in there and I'll let you get back to sleep."

Shiva wasn't sure what to make of this but the last thing he wanted to do was to prolong this contact with what he considered dangerous and arbitrary authority.

"Sweet, get my pouch and give it to this officer."

By the time Sweet had given him the pouch, the man had unlocked Shiva's handcuffs and was heading for his cruiser.

Shiva and Sweet just looked at each other.

"Let's go back to bed."

"Yea…"

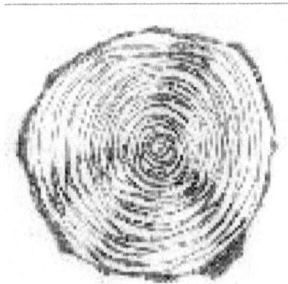

4

Grandiose Hotel

Morning came with the sun already over the coastal hills. Small shafts of light were shooting through worn, slightly torn curtains hanging in the van windows. Out of the softness of the aqua blue sheepskins Sweet opened one eye and let the light play with her ambivalent thoughts, *What a strange night, where was I? Dreaming again? Still dreaming?* "Shiva, Shiva, hey, it's morning, where..." Nudging him, without any response, she got up and climbed over him until she fell out of the front right door, rolled over and breathed deeply several times, letting the night fade into oblivion. She could feel it. The morning was filling her lungs to a breaking point. She could feel her body coming alive..."Shiva, come out here, it's, like, wow, breathe it in..."

Shiva poked his head out, sniffed the air and let his eyes widen. For the first time they took in the street, the whitewashed building on the corner, with its bell tower, looked like the village church. Next to it was a wooden wall with bougainvillea flowing over it. A chain-link gate led to an old cottage and a yard that bordered a driveway with someone hauling out odd things - furniture, books - to put on the front lawn. They both looked up and began to laugh at the sign over the door, which was much too large for the building, but then again maybe there was something they didn't know about. The sign, a huge monstrosity that was probably left over from a bankrupt old mining town, read *Grandiose Hotel*. Now, this relic was gracing an old two-story wood frame house that looked like it had been in Bolinas from the beginning of its village days.

"Grandiose Hotel," Shiva chimed with an overstated French touch. "Perhaps we should peruse the fine antiques?"

Shiva," Sweet spoke wistfully, "did we have a visitor last night?"

"Sweet, I vaguely recall that we had to give up some of our spiritual smoke in order to stay here. But, it will all be for the good. The man in question needs enlightenment more than we do."

"Shiva, what about enlightenment? What is it that we have that he doesn't have?"

"Sweet, wow, is this a time for a discourse on enlightenment?" With this question his eyes grew large and then he cocked his head, smiled an impish smile and said, "Or shall we concern ourselves with material things?"

She smiled and continued to question with her gaze.

"Alright, let's start with enlightenment. From our childhood beginnings, our senses began to define the world outside of us. As we continued to define the outside world we began to question and it is that very important conscious questioning that, ironically, began to create our beginning awareness and shall we say, later on, awareness of our beginning. We come from sources much thought about in our history. Some have called those sources spiritual angelic beings, some people still believe in Genesis as a literal happening, some have thought that we dreamed ourselves into being or that we have emanated out of idealized, formative, forming principles or that we have come out of energized paths…and many people throughout history have added to our layers of awareness - from Lao Tzu to Plato to Meister Eckhart to Hamlet to Kant to Rudolf Steiner to Heisenberg to Buckminster Fuller. They have all added to our enlightenment, to the dance, the on-going dance of life…

"Shiva, woe, slowdown, I think you've lost me, I don't know half those people…"

"Sweet, I don't know their personal lives that well but I know them through their ideas – primarily from what I've read and taken in. For example, Lao Tzu lived about 2600 years ago. He wrote the Tao Te Ching, which essentially says that all the different things of the universe are all manifestations of an interconnected unity. Now Plato lived about 100 years afterwards and he flourished during the Greek classical age. He's known for his philosophical writings, many of which use dialogue as a way of getting at the truth of personal and cultural issues, including virtue and justice and knowledge. Meister Eckhart lived in the 14th century, he was a Dominican monk and spoke of the mysteries of life. I can talk more about the others but this approach is not the only way to

24

know the past."

"What do you mean?"

"Well, hold on to your beads, Sweet, I'll tell you what Rudolf Steiner, who was an esoteric twentieth century philosopher, thought, he thought the spiritual history of life on earth, or maybe of the universe, is somehow written or recorded on something called the akashic record and I'm not talking about a greatest hits album, even though that record could be the greatest of all time. Imagine, Sweet, somewhere, out there, is a record of all the thoughts and events that have ever occurred and, here's the wildest part of all, you can tune into it. At least, that's what Steiner thought and supposedly, with clairvoyance, he did tune into this. As a result his world view of prehistory - the time not written down, came alive through his tuning into this record."

"Shiva, I think I need some juice. Can we get some breakfast? "

"Sure, you definitely need a good breakfast with Steiner."

We left the VW and walked across the street to the Grandiose Hotel.

There was a nod from the man hauling out a bookshelf. He was wearing a paisley vest that looked like something from my grandmother's couch. His hair was tied back into a ponytail and he seemed to take great pains with each item.

"Mornin."

"Good morning, we were just admiring your sign and getting hungry and..." Sweet rambled on, "What we were wondering is, if there is a bakery around here, for a pastry or something?"

"Actually, there's one around the corner. It is in the old house off the street, go past the library and between two large palms.

"Thanks, by the way, what's the story of the Grandiose Hotel? Do you actually have rooms...? "

"Yes, we do, two of them, with kitchen facilities."

"Can we take a look? I mean..."

"We happen to have one available. Are you interested? "

"We might be. We were rudely confronted by a local deputy last night."

"Oh yeah, that was probably Roderick, he's a pain but he doesn't come around that often, it's just that he doesn't have a regular Schedule."

"Probably, when his stash runs low."

"So, you got to know him."

"Well, we may want to sleep through the night. What's your name? "

"I'm Val, we, that is Natalie and I, run this place. Come on, I'll show you the room, it's the front one over the sign."

We walked out back through a rickety Screen door past the washer and dryer into the kitchen up the stairs into a refurbished remodeled attic-like room which had an assortment of odd and old pieces of furniture that Val must have collected over the years.

"I love this room, Shiva, let's stay here let's, let's..."

"Is it available? "

"Yes, right now, someone cancelled. I'm looking for a longer term person though."

"How long?"

"A week or a month."

"Well, how much for a week?"

"Thirty-nine dollars."

"Sounds good, we'll take it."

"Okay, let's sign you up."

They followed Val to the old cash register in the store where Shiva handed him two 20s and signed something with carbon paper in it.

"We're in." He looked at Sweet as she pulled and tugged at him to go back upstairs.

"A whole week, this is gonna be great, wow."

They climbed the narrow staircase again, opened the door and slowly looked around. Shiva was drawn to the light, went straight to the window and turned the worm gears that opened the windows outwards.

5

Two Roads

As the windows opened, the glass panes reflected a changing scenery. *Was it from the outside or the inside? Was his mind playing tricks?* Shiva couldn't tell. Without thinking, he closed his eyes, breathed deeply, until a litany of images rose up, between the windows and his mind, a street scene was forming…He heard Robert Frost's voice, *two roads diverged in a wood…*Incredibly, he was standing there, yet, also moving towards a divergence. From his one view whole view he started going down both streets. He could feel the pull. He could smell the overweight air of one street, hung over, slowing down, dissolving…He could smell the rising perfume of the other street, drawing him in…Each doorway beckoned, the street narrowed and clouded over with orange and turquoise batik sheets to help keep out the heat, baskets lined the walls of cracked stucco. "Tea, hot tea…" a voice came from around the corner. A tall, lean middle-aged man in a caftan entered the narrow alley, holding a brass tray over his head, on which were balanced several small brass cups and a tall thin spouted pitcher. He swayed past the baskets and people in his way, "Tea, hot tea, the best of Ceylon."

"Yes, I'll take some," he said, and sat down at a small table near several other men ensconced nearby, probably locals. In a rhythmic movement, not missing a beat, the tea purveyor proceeded to set up the cup and saucer, poured the tea and inquired in English, "You would like it sweet?"

"Yes."

Yes, I would like it just the way it is, I would like it sweet but my mood is sour, burnt, devastated...I have this strange despair...With this confession the spell broke, the scene dissolved and Shiva was no longer in the café, his feet were on the other avenue, a street of pain, with a deep upwelling of anxious angst, without any understanding of why and where it came from, this was the other side, the other street... where the air punctuated his nostrils until he coughed, almost violently, until he doubled over looking into the haggard face of someone's forgotten soul...

"You got it bad, honey, " she rasped.

Turning red from coughing, it seemed he was the one dying. "I'll, I'll be all right, hac cak cough..." but the stench didn't let up. His eyes watered until she was hazy, until even the broken cement became indistinct and softer, until he simply rolled over next to this layer of aromas and blankets and patches of clothing reeking, yet, surprisingly warm, even soft, soothing..."I am lost in it..." he cried in utter shame and loss..."I am lost in her world..."

She has seen me before, she has seen more than she will ever let on. Her eyes have conditioned, maybe permanent, layers of too many bygone goodbyes. She is weary and takes me in only to feel me in places where the possibility of some hard cash can be found, the jiggle of coins, a wad of bills...but all she can feel is a growing hunger...

"Just hold me, lady, lady midnight, just hold me for a minute just for a..." His voice was no longer his, his voice was no longer...his body was no longer solid no longer solid...wanting for it all to end..."just hold me..."

He undoes his belt and takes her hand, her fingers, her wrist and pushes her into his loosened pants, down deep into his hunger.

It has begun to rain but he feels nothing, nothing but her fingers crawling around inside him, tightening around him, until she holds on.

"Is this what you want, eh, my lost child."

He knows she is mocking him

"How much do you want? "

"I want out of the rain. I what all you've got." She gets on her knees to stand up, the blanket falls, her patches move, she stands up holding onto his growing hunger, his hopeful redemption.

"C'mon." surprisingly, her strength pulls him up. They stagger into the nearest dimly lit doorway with a *Rooms to Let* sign. He knocks until a small window slides open.

"Yes."

"Have you got a room for the night?" The eyes in the window darted back and forth.

"No, we're full."

They moved to the next shabby front lobby. The manager looks at them. With disgust on his face he sneered, "get out."

"This is crazy! He thinks. The rain was beating on them incessantly, soaking him until there was no distinction between his shirt and body, his eyes search for another haven somewhere, to where she can, she can, satiate this hunger, anywheeeeere…

The lights of a taxi approach, he jumps up, she lets go of him, he stops the taxi and opens the back door. He jumps in and pulls her to him.

"Up the street!" he orders, "just drive up the street."

Out of the rain they both breathe in, safe at last; forever. They are in darkness except for the recurring streetlights. She wants the money, he wants her, but it is too obvious, the cab driver is looking. She is distracted. She says, "Stop at the Hotel Mirage. I know who runs it." They stop. He pays the driver. They go to the window. "Any rooms?" she asks.

"We're full tonight."

"Any room anywhere? We just need to go the bathroom."

He looks at them, sees the desperation. They will pay for their hunger.

"40 bucks. No more than an hour."

He pays and they are let in, out of the rain, out of the unknown, to a third floor bathroom, down the hall. They enter the darkly lit stall; he pushes her head down and pulls at his belt, his pants. She holds him with her left hand, feeling him with her right.

"This is what you want." she says, and feels him, feels his pocket, pulling on him while she thrusts her right hand into his pocket grabs his wallet and throws it on the floor, now into his pants pocket until she has a wad of bills.

"This is what I want." she whispers to him, going faster, his eyes are shut, oblivious to all before him and after him. Suddenly, she let's go and bursts out of the stall. Holding only the wad of bills, she runs down the hall leaving him in unrelieved agony. His eyes open and he stumbles out only to see her running, between yellowed, pitted, replastered walls, the hall they came in is now a turningtwisted alley, with the echo of her laughter subsiding, dying, soaking into the old weatherworn bricks and stones…He is back now, his pants are again tightly belted, he is drinking his sweetened tea in the open café…around the corner of the narrow alley he had taken out of curiosity, alienated curiosity – there, but not there, hearing, seeing, taking up physical space yet somehow separate from the surroundings, until a young voice breaks in, "You are from America? "

A yellow-toothed boy is standing next to him.

"What?" he half smiles at him.

"You are from America? "

"No, I come from Germany." For some reason that he doesn't understand, he hides his American ness.

"Oh, Sie kommen aus Deutschland."

"Ya, aber ich spreche English."

"Yes, my English better," the boy says, "Deutschland good education."

"Yes."

"My cousin learn there. He is engineer."

"Where is he now?"

"He's here, in Cairo. He drives a taxi, No work here. I have other family, make fine wooden boxes."

"Aha."

"I take you there. No one hassle you. You go with me. I show you good work."

"Ya, what family?"

"Come, I show you good work. My cousin has box factory."

He smiled and the boy smiled wider showing brown left over teeth with eyes blazing. He took my hand and we meandered through the alleys, turning left right left under ancient archways, along built over walls, to a door to a small room with at least six people busy drilling sawing gluing sanding and polishing small boxes with inlaid wood and hinged covers with felt on the inside. He handed me several.

"Here, good work."

They stopped to see my response.

"You sure this is a cousin of yours?" I said while opening the top of one box after another. One closed softly beautifully with a suction that made me feel like I could put a ring of lapis lazuli in it or an ancient Scarab carved out of amber and it would be safe and secure as long as I kept it in the box.

"This is nice work," I offered.

"Yes, very nice," the cousin responded.

"Very low price too."

"Oh yeah, how much?"

"Two pounds."

"Wow, that's a lot." He remembered that you never take the first offer; that you have to bargain.

"OK, for you, one pound."

"Better, but I'm not sure."

"OK, OK, last price, one-half pound."

"You got it." That was my first purchase. I guess he knew he had me hooked because he proceeded to take me to his other cousins and brothers and uncles that day. By the time we sat down again for a tea and a hookah I had a bag full of specialty items made by the local craftsman, made by hands handed down for hundreds of years – embroidered pillow slips, an embossed brass plate, rose attar. Laden with my bazaar bag of bargained crafts and my camera and a Perrier, I wandered deeper into the maze of alleyways. I told Ahmed that I needed to explore by myself and left him with a somewhat sad look which may have coincided with a loss look – a loss of a free-spending tourist who he thought came from Germany, In fact, he told me, I was not at all like other Germans. "They hang onto their pennies." he said, "They don't

bargain! You," shaking his head up and down, "you know good quality."
Well, I guess I did. I had a bagful. But shadows had fallen down the
walls and over the cobble stones of every narrow alley way I turned into,
feeling my way down and along built over and over walls with ancient
doors on every side. Occasionally a sound could be heard but its source
was vague, echoing off the hard sandstone. In this shadowed
reverberating world I imagine the sounds, even the voices seeping out of
the ground, even the walls oozing out of millennia - voices in Arabic and
Hebraic toiling in the searing sun, voices of anguish. My ears cocked to
every sound, my eyes darting - I notice a movement, someone, Jesus, I
hold onto my camera...
"Hello," I call out.
"Hello," someone calls back.
"Do you speak English?"
"Yes, American,"
"Yes."
I see an older man, with a furrowed face, not tall, in a caftan.
"You are lost."
"Yes, no, I'm not sure...I want to get back..."
"You are American, an American lost in these old paths.
"Yes, it seems that way."
"You are close to freedom"
"What do you mean?"
"We live in darkness, in shadows, in the past. We live in this maze and
continue to go down one path after another. We know the twists and
turns, we drink the tea, we smoke the hookahs, we talk of America...we
see *Shane*...we see the good, the bad and the ugly...someone told me
you want to go to the moon..."
"Well, that's not me."
"You have money, you are rich."
"No, I have enough for this."
"You can leave here and talk of our past and go into the future."
"I don't know. I can't seem to find my way out."
"Then you are doomed to stay here and wander through these streets
forever. You can sell your camera."
"Hey, come on, there has to be a way out, a way back?"
"Can you go forward by going back?"
"No, yes, no, sometimes."
"Well, can you? That's the question. Can you use the past to go forward,
Mr. America?"
"Sure, you use the past to learn, to remember, to..."
"And what have you learned?"
"I've got an education, I graduated from the university."
"And what have you learned?"
"I graduated in the Humanities. I learned about the world's ideas, it's
arts."
"Ah, so you have read about us."

"Yes, well, not really. I studied ancient Egypt – the beginnings of civilization."

"So now you think you know us, do you?"

"Well real people, the real world is a little more complex, or let me say, immediate."

"Yes, that is a way of saying it. You have, at least, the beginnings of learning. In your days of wandering through this maze what have the people told you?"

"Well," I blinked and fell momentarily silent, "People live here, their life is here, they aren't going anywhere else. This is their home, their work. They are part of the walls it seems, no, they are in between, they hold the walls up...I heard children's voices behind curtains, I saw a man, an embroiderer, he looked like he'd been sitting there his whole life, his body had conformed to sitting on pillows while embroidering Islamic designs onto one pillow slip after another. I bought a pillowcase from him. I'm going to take it home. It looks like he can't move. He is rooted to his skill and allotted a small space to work in and be in...and probably has been there for centuries. A boy, in the nook of a wall, convinced me I needed a shoeshine. I put my shoe on his wooden box. He looked at me with the deepest brown eyes, grinned and spoke through yellow teeth, *I make shoes shine*."

I asked him if he spoke English. He said yes and German and Italian and French. I asked him if he had been to those countries. He said he learned the language from all the visitors. He had never been out of the Sook."

"You have learned much, Mr. America, now I ask you why do people stay here in this small crowded, broken-down built up place?"

I wanted to be concise and profound. I thought and answered him, "because this place is their home, it's your home."

The old man smiled slightly and nodded his head in a pleased manner, like a teacher who just seen his a student achieve an insight into a problem.

"He can learn," he thought, "this American can learn."

"But," he continued with a question for the old man, "how do you leave your home to go after something else?"

"How do we leave the past that we live in? Is that what you want to know? "

"Yes, I think so."

"You have answered and your answer has given truth to the question. It is a question for this time. Just as I call you Mr. America, I know that you come from a country of immigrants, people who have all left their homes of some kind, like these, like others, for many reasons they left to go into the future, mostly with only hope and dreams to guide them and this is ingrained in Americans. You have a tremendous vitality to push towards the future. Now, you go back into the world, sometimes reluctantly, come back here and we know you as Captain America or Charlie Chaplin or 'The call of the wild' or as Rawhide or Queen for a day or Elvis Presley or the Grand Canyon or the men on the moon or, he paused, the mushroom cloud..."

"That's American culture and technology."

"And American might."

"There are some ideas to go with all that."

"Yes, with all that we have a window to see America, a window that gets bigger all time, a window for Ahmed and the shoeshine boy, even the embroiderer."

"What can I do?"

"You are part of the window."

"Yes, yes."

"At some point, sometime, you will wonder why there is envy or even hatred of America and our black gold will fuel that hatred and envy.

"Look, I am here because of my circumstance and you are here because of yours. We're both going into the future..." As he said this, I wondered at his own particular predicament and asked the old man, "Is there a way out?"

They let this question linger as the sounds of honking horns permeated the darkened alley. The old man took him by the arm and led him along the smoothed surface of a high wall. They turned until a narrow sliver of light became wider. In a soft voice he told me, "For you, there is a way out, at least for now." and brought me to an opening in the wall, a doorway, as old as the Sook, a doorway that opened to a wide thoroughfare of the city...the ancientmodern city of Cairo. His eyes closed to the light, his ears opened to the noise, the cacophony of the world...

6

Surfer

"Shiva, are we going to get a pastry?" A simple question brought him back from his inner separation, his inner wandering. Wavering, holding on to the top of the open windows, finally letting go enough to let his fingers slide down to the metal hardware designed to open and close them, hoping to close them, his fingers were unable to grip, wanting to close them, wanting one window again, one window to see out of and to see in...

"Sweet," his voice was swollen with emotion, "Sweet, we're all one, we're all one," he repeated, "yet sometimes...sometimes, it seems like we travel down various roads all at the same time. We're all one and we have the inner capacity to travel along any number of roads... Think about it Sweet, there are many roads inside us, from earliest living things to complex evolutionary reminders, our brains recapitulate the reptilian and the mammalian until we get to..." he stopped and took a deep breath before he continued, "until we get to this vessel that contains years of nurturing and socializing and accumulating...constantly trying to reconcile the opposites, as it extends it's reach..."

When he finally opened his eyes he was rotating the worm gear hardware, turning the windows inward until they touched. The room filled with a quiet he had almost forgotten was possible. He lay down on the high brass bed, lost in thought, oblivious to Sweet closing the door behind her. The old staircase creaked several times as she descended, took a look around the kitchen, fondled the teabags in a small basket - Lemon Zinger - *I could use a cup of that*, she thought, but left it for later. *I think I wanna see the beach; I wanna feel the sand…a pastry can wait.* She went out of the back door, down the driveway and headed left, walking lightly on the road between the mesas. She could smell the ocean, the heavy smell of dying drying seaweed spewed upon the beach, the smell of salty decay…it only drew her closer. *This was the Pacific, after all, somewhere out there is Hawaii*, she thought, *somewhere over there is Japan, somewhere, somewhere is the rest of the world, only now, here, I am filling my lungs with the ionized air made possible by this unimaginable watery presence…*

"Hey, how's it going?" A wet suited surfer had caught up with her.

"Hey, OK."

His blond hair was draped over the black back of the wet suit. His bare feet were looking for smooth pavement to walk on. As they both neared the narrow decline to the beach she noticed the sea wall on their right. It had a spray-painted peace sign on it with rainbow colors shooting out of it becoming stripes along the wall which guided her eyes to the vista of the ocean opening up to them, the surf washing towards them…

"Looking good." his eyes widen as he spoke, "Are you visiting or…?"

"Yea, I, that is we, just came here yesterday. A friend of mine and I are staying at the hotel down the street."

"Where?"

"The Grandiose Hotel, right down the street…with the used clothing store and bookstore in the front. We have a great room, overlooking the street right over the sign."

"They actually have rooms? I thought the sign was just a joke, though he does have some good stuff, sometimes. I bought a guitar from him last year.

"Yea"

"And, not only that, we're playing tonight at the Community Center. Come on by."

"Where's that? "

"By the gas station, around the corner. Well, I'm heading in."

"OK, hey…" Crashing waves obscured her voice as she watched him walk into the surf, straddle his surfboard and paddle out. Her eyes eventually let him go, as he became part of the constantly changing patterns on the surface of the water. She looked westward to see the beach narrow along the base of the cliffs, while a glow of light outlined the furthest point of the mesa. She turned and looked eastward to see the folds of Tamalpais fall into the Bolinas lagoon. The midday sun was beginning to turn her dress into a golden blanket with greenblack oaks accentuating the undulations of her hills.

She walked towards them, weaving in and out with the waves. She could see another beach, across the inlet of the Bolinas lagoon. Right now she felt strangely separated from the other side of the inlet, not just physically but inwardly, she couldn't really explain it, yet there something about this beach itself that made her feel different. Maybe it was the cliffs hovering over her, looking like they were in a constant possibility of falling. The sandstone piles at the base were evidence of the water and wind erosion. A home on top of the Mesa had half a gazebo protruding over the top of the cliff, ominously warning all who walked underneath. This in-between of sand and waves, having the possibility of rearranging the very ground she walked on, gave her a heightened feeling of awareness. If she lay down, she wondered how long before the cliff would fall on her or a wave would cover her. She felt this dynamic on the beach of Bolinas and yet she accepted it, felt it, and eventually found a great weathered log to put her head on. The air was still and warm. She felt alone, took off her shoes and socks, rolled up her pants and in an impetuous moment took off her T-shirt. She didn't wear a bra and loved feeling the air on her young breasts. She lay down and let the elements lull her, the slight breeze caress her. Time had stopped for her. Only the comments of two momentary beachcombers drifted her way.

7

Schilling and Damian

"…Definitely not in Detroit anymore…"

"A little slice of Eden, my friend."

"Am I seeing right or has Eve returned to this godforsaken garden?"

"Eve has returned to this godforsaken garden."

"What is youth, my friend, but a young woman in all her budding beauty."?

"And young men, what of them, are they not a part of this diorama?"

"You put it in perspective. We were the young men, and now we can enjoy this scene of possibility."

"Not my possibility."

"What do you mean?"

"Too much beer has shaped me into a spectator."

"Not age?"

"Beer and age."

"Not a bad combination. You have, however, exercised your mind over the years."

"Well, that does bring about an appreciation of the finer things."

"You have always idealized life."

"Why do you think I've spent half my life in bars?"

"Because of it's ideal environment."

"Because I could not live with the realization."

"Now you're becoming abstruse."

"The pain of realization, my friend, that I will always be something less than the ideal."

"Allow yourself some consolation or appreciation."

"I have allowed it. When I was in Greece I strolled around the Parthenon two times. Even in its 2500-year-old state of being I was moved to tears. I've also seen the magnificent marble statues taken off the pedestal by Lord Elgin. I imagined them above me again playing out their mythical roles. Yes, I do appreciate a culture that not only idealized the physical human being but also recreated it. It is an incredible legacy for all of us."

"We both know the history that brought those people to such artistic levels – we know the Egyptian influence – we know that their free standing sculpture went from the stance of the Koori to the spear thrower to the dying warrior to the... we could go on, but needless to say, the artistic ability of those sculptor's achievements are still without parallel..."

"And they are still with us, as reminders."

"Yes, but can we live with them?"

"Even now, they are a sacrilege to some religious groups – over the ages the Christians whacked off the penises and despoiled the breasts, and then Mohammed, literally, made any image of God a sacrilege."

"Yes, just as religious zealots have destroyed statues, one image after the other has perished."

"But in the process, Islamic art took abstract design to a higher level, just consider their calligraphy."

"Not to mention the Persian miniatures, but does one have to be destroyed in order to facilitate the other?"

"Well, there is the explanation of the Hindu god – *the lord of the dance* – who dances out the creation of the world and then gets tired and allows destruction to follow, which mythologically explains it."

"There is also the idea of the *Phoenix* – the mythical bird that self-immolates after turning its nest into a funeral pyre and after three days rises again and becomes this new and beautiful bird. Our history has shown that humans need to transcend their experience of destruction – one mythology after another makes an attempt to explain the destructive forces people have had to live through, or rather, die through. We still marvel and wonder at their resurgence and their rebirth out of the ashes – out of Dresden...and Hiroshima... and who know what future crucible of destruction that begets a rebirth..."

"We've come a long way, baby."

"And now, we have to explain the hydrogen bomb? This star force on the earth that our intelligence was able to decipher and then recreate, here, on the earth. Is there a mythological explanation for this?"

"We could blame Prometheus for it."

"Actually, the more important question is how…"

"How do we keep from blowing ourselves up?"

"That's why we've imagined *the lord of the dance* and *Brahma*, the creator, and also the possibility of resurrection through the Christ mythos…"

"Or, we could appeal to most people's will to live? I mean, even if we can't appeal to those sick human aberrations who believe they will be heroes in another life if they destroy others and die in the process…most people want to live…"

"Yes, we better continue to appeal and educate, because…we want…" he paused and reflected, "what other choice do we have?"

"Interestingly, and understandably, and too often, unfortunately, for most people, these man-made destructive forces - those suicide bombers and future button pushers - are just out there somewhere, and just become an abstraction, unless, of course, you've become a target."

"Most people pretty much live day-to-day lives, assuming nothing will happen - that includes earthquakes and tornadoes and tsunamis."

"And those used to be 'acts of God or gods'."

"I think we have digressed enough. Let us put our minds back on the beach."

With this last remark they found their way out of their mental labyrinth and stood in the doorway of their senses, feeling light grains of sand blowing on their faces. The breeze had intensified and the sky had darkened over them leaving only a low luminous orangeyellow strip on the western horizon. They both turned their heads to avoid the sand and noticed the hills in the east had turned a deep violet from the sun's last gasp. Strangely, there was no thought of a metaphoric mountain princess for them, only the realization that the hills would all turn into shades of gray if they gazed at them long enough. They were lost in the twilight, just as the young woman was lost to them. She had left while they had pondered the abstract realizations of destruction and rebirth.

"Our glimpse of Eden has vanished," Schilling said to Damian.

"Yes, somehow banished from our site."

"Let us find a suitable eating establishment to continue this conversation."

"I think we may have to take what we can get," Damian responded, his voice falling into a rolling wave.

They continued on their shoreline stroll extracting general ideas from the particular. Schilling was a muttonchops rotund Falstaff and Damian, constantly pushing his glasses up, was his traveling companion. They had both left their homes and studies in Michigan to take a short sojourn in California.

"A reality check," they had both thought. "What was all the fuss about, anyway?" They weren't planning on wearing flowers in their hair but they were impressed with the youthful outpouring they had seen on the beach. And this beach, they had noticed, was not a vast stretch of almost virgin granules of fine sand, like the one across the tidal entrance of the

41

lagoon. No, this was a dirty play land of washed up flotsam and jetsam and ashes from forgotten fires and seaweed and falling cliffs. You could walk the short beach journey from the main road Sweet had taken to the other side of the beach, onto a road that followed the lagoon inland. Here, houses, built on stilts, next to the road, stayed above the incessant tidal sea level fluctuations, and curved around the contour of the high Mesa. It was not the kind of beach you would take a fastidious mother to, but for those who wanted to build a fire, roast sandy hot dogs, walk on hot ashes or have five live dogs follow you around, this beach nurtured the unexpected. Today it was Schilling and Damian's time to find it. As they crossed the breakwater, a cement barrier, about two feet wide, going from the base of the cliffs out into the surf, their heads turned towards a strange amalgamation of found materials below the cliffs. Four, roughly ten feet high, assemblages could be seen, two with, what looked like, makeshift guitars, one that looked like a drummer with arms raised high and finally a sax player. The quartet imposed themselves on all those who wandered by. Driftwood, tires, rope, old clothes, abalone shells and long scarves brought this local, larger than life band to life. They played with the wind while an offbeat bass crashed on the shore…

8

Sweet Smoke

"Gentleman, you've obviously come for the concert." A voice could be heard coming from the shanty standing near the assembled figures. They looked for signs of life but found only the darkened door of a makeshift hogan. "Do not look for more, gentleman, for I offer you the spirit of the music. As my grandfather used to say, *music is for those who have ears connected to the earth.* This band plays for all who have the ears, more than that, all who have the heart to hear it. Listen, gentlemen, even the seagulls join in."

Schilling turned a quizzical eye towards Damian and they both looked up to see sea gulls perched on the arms and heads of the band, their movements bringing about a high pitched tinkling of abalone shells as the solid whump of a drum beat joined in with a steady rhythm...

"Ahhhhhohhhhhhhhawwwwww..." a lone voice spilled out of the hogan, adding to the accompaniment and spreading out around them.

The sound harkened back to Indian chanting they had heard on TV westerns, yet, there was something about the bass voice and the persistent drumbeat, the heavy beat that created an underlying mood.

The more they listened the more palpable a mood of detachment came over them. After some time, Schilling felt, or imagined he felt, that the sand was vibrating to the evoking sound. He touched the beach with his hand. The motion was noticeable. He beckoned Damian over to him, put his hand on his shoulder and urged him to bend down to feel the pulsating grains moving around them. A seagull screeched as if to warn them but they only felt motion. They had both heard of the San Andreas fault and for a moment considered that this was going to be the 'big one', the earthquake that would send them all packing, hippies, bikers, new-agers, gurus, maybe not old-timers, but they weren't sure…their sojourn on the beach had, at least, put them on some wavelength that opened them up to the vibrating grains of a sands dancing in front of them. They were not in a position to judge the rationality of it. The sweet smoke that came from the rolledup joint Hollywood had contributed to their meeting; that they were passing back and forth, made judgment unnecessary (Was it a projection of popular fiction ala Castaneda or illusions or delusions or too much sun, that made them question solid ground). As the waves whooshed and pounded an irregular rhythm to the thump thump thump of the drum there was movement above them, the band had come to life! At least it looked like the metal musicians were moving and joining in.

"It could all be explained away," Schilling thought, while one guitarist jiggled his legs, "it could all be explained away," yet the accumulating effect transcended their ability to explain it away - they were transfixed - the sand kept sparkling off the last rays of the setting sun, creating one image after another - the wheel of life eventually changed into an ancient interlocking design that they knew only too well. Time had stood still for them. Shadows had taken over their vision and variegated grays had supplanted any left over violet hues. With their whole beings poised, the accumulated movements and sounds penetrated the growing darkness and spoke to them on other levels, while an evening fog descended and poured over the sounding surf, becoming a hovering mist, obscuring the cliff and the beach. Looking up they noticed colored movement, brown and gold fluttering, through the haze, as if attached to some ethereal being - a moving gliding being…They were caught up in it, momentarily transfixed, and yet, they slowly began to feel the cold, moist air; feel it penetrate their clothes until they were naked, waiting… waiting for respite…this time a seagull's screeching answered their call, finally breaking the spell; bringing them back. Looking around for familiar signs, they saw the bulky figure of Hollywood hunched over his drum and lifted their eyes, again, to the brown and gold movement of a scarf against the sky. As they continued to gaze up, the mist cleared just enough to see that the Milky Way had emerged in all its possibilities, bringing them back to solid earth. Walking and stumbling over the beach they carefully and haphazardly stepped over and around the breakwater boulders at the end of it and finally put their feet onto the road. From there they strode in silence until the noise from Smileys met them halfway.

44

9

Bear and sidekick

"Goddamn those kids, man. They're gonna fuck up this town."
"Maybe we should roust them out, round them up, *Rawhiiiiide*...the high note of Rawhide resounded over the din of the smoke-filled bar room of Smileys, just as Schilling and Damian strode through the swinging doors. Beer guzzling laughter and leatherjackets greeted them as they tried to find space at the bar. One heavy bearded rollicking Hell's Angel type, with obvious relish, graciously moved aside to let them step up.
"Gentleman," he spoke with a faint dignity, "I gather you're not from around here?"
Schilling, in his tweed jacket, cautiously nodded, after the experience on the beach, this rough and ready environment brought both of them out of any left over ethereal stupor. After a pause Shilling finally said, "We're visiting."
"Staying here, actually." Damian added.
"Act u al ly," was syllabically pronounced by the bearded man.
"Yes," Damian answered, "we thought we would take in the ambiance of this coastal village, so to speak."

"So to speak, you say. I guess you are…"

"So to speaking…hahhahhah…" His belly laugh swept down the bar. Damian looked at Schilling, raised his eyebrows to signal some concerted response. "I do believe we've come to the right place," Schilling spoke, looking at Damian but making sure the burly man heard. Finally, leaning over to him, he quietly said, "Can we take you into our confidence? We are actually doing research here. A sociological study for a Midwest university."

The man just shook his head. "Don't fuck with me guys."

"Look, you are obviously a local here and we're interested in the latest sociological trends. Maybe you have some ideas."

"What!"

"What is at the core of this so-called 'hippie' movement? I mean something is going on…

"But you don't know what it is, do you, Mr. Jones." Another patron, who had been listening, added a current lyric to the conversation.

"These guys are doing research on the hippies."

"Jesus, they've got some nerve. We're just talking about rounding them up when you walked in."

"We could brand them."

"That's a good idea. That way, we could round them up anytime we want. That is, if they get out of control."

"Schilling finally got a word in, "Gentlemen, you have a certain flair for individuality."

They both looked at him.

"I mean you seem to be doing your own thing? What do you make of all these young people coming to California and *doing their own thing*?"

The bearded man looked at them and then turned to his friend at the bar, "Sidekick, these guys are either on the level, or they think they're talking to a couple of patsies in here."

"Bear, I don't like to be considered a patsy."

"I see, gentleman, maybe we could continue this at another time. We've just come in to wet our whistle, so to speak."

"*So to speak*, he says," with a broad smile coming back on Bear's face, "Look you guys are all right. Here lemme buy you a beer."

"Well, that's not necessary."

"But we'll take your offer, thanks."

"If you'll let us reciprocate some time."

"What did he say?" Sidekick said to Bear with a questioning look.

"He said he'll buy us a beer some time."

"Alright, I'll drink to that."

They lifted their glasses in the midst of smoke and the sharp crack of a cue ball breaking the pack.

"Here's to women," Bear said to the three faces looking at him.

"And to Harleys." His friend added.

"And those who mount them." Bear finished the toast creating a barrage of laughter from the bar. Schilling and Damian were unsure of the humor

46

but were more relieved that these locals had taken them in. In this case 'taken in' meant being accepted into their bar scene, into their humor, instead of the result of their humor or the butt of their joke. When you're laughing with them, there's an acceptance. That's the way Schilling and Damian felt and decided it might be a good time to take a breather.

"Gentlemen, I feel it's time for us to enjoy a repast at your venerable restaurant."

"What did he say?"

"He said, they're gonna grab something to eat."

"It's been a privilege," Damian said, as he nodded goodbyes.

"Can we continue this?"

"We'll be here." Both Bear and Sidekick responded.

10

Rosa

They stepped out of the ruckus of Smileys and let the evening air refresh them, let them breathe in the cool ocean air, until they were buoyed and invigorated and walking brightly across the street to the Shoppe, the only restaurant open for dinner that they could see. Scowleys had closed for the day and Mariah had gone to the Community Center for the weekly open mike. They walked in and settled into a corner, surrounded by a window on one side and a potbellied stove on the other. Next to the stove were bookshelves with enough reading material to take the edge off the slow service. While waiting for the waitress, who was handsome, Schilling perused the bookshelf and pulled out a defrayed and worn out book, *Mysteries of the San Francisco Bay Area*. He read the title to himself and pulled it off the shelf. Always looking for the unusual, he thought it might shed some light on their weird experience on the beach. Even if his rational mind could eliminate that, he still had a penchant for serendipitous connections.

"I may have found a door to this strange world, Damian," he spoke, adding his customary uproarious laugh at the end. Sitting down again, he opened the book and read the first line that his eager eyes fell on, "The stone world came to me, and said, 'Flesh gives you an hour's life'." It was a quote from Gregory Corso supposedly remembered by Allen Ginsberg and finally resurrected in a book called *The Beach Hotel*.

"That is a line, Damian. I don't think we have to go any further." He read it again, slowly, with an emphasis on *stone* and *flesh*. "So, here we have the first layered meaning of the evening, my friend. The *stone world* is personified – alive – and speaks to this Corso. *Stone* usually refers to a lifeless world in which are grains of sand and yet, this world speaks. Is that any different from our experience on the beach? And what does this world tell him: that *flesh* - blood and guts and all - has given him an hour's life."

"Yes," Damian added, "And what did our experience tell us, that we had a rare moment, maybe a nonlinear moment, of some illusory reality? I thought I heard something and, and we both saw the mist…"

Schilling did not want to continue in that direction and brought them back to the quote, "*Flesh* has taken on meaning – both living and allegorical - but first, it is a word and a word that came out of a random flipping of the pages among many words on the page. It was strung together with other words, including *stone*, in a poetic and, still, coherent manner. So, we could say, meaning has come from not just the word flesh and stone, but also from the phrasing or literate context they are couched in."

"Schilling, I hesitate to add that you are roaming in a field of abstractions here and getting awfully close to deconstructing the language. Is there a particular meaning you want to illuminate?"

"Damian, again, you are trying to get to a point that, once achieved, is not fully thought through…Is mental exploration not the path that extends our understanding; that brings us knowledge; that let's us float our ideas, that…"

"What'll it be, gents?"

"Ah, now there's an idea."

"We don't have that on the menu."

"What?"

"Ideas."

"You're out?"

"We rarely get them in here."

"In any case, frozen, not fresh."

"Flesh?"

"Fresh, now maybe you need some more time?"

"Ah, now that's a relative thought"

"Idea?"

"No, uncle."

"I give up."

"Look, I'll bring you some water. Our specials are on the board or maybe you'd like to read the menu? If that's not too down to earth."

"I believe she has a point."

"I think we're back to where we started. Shall we peruse the menu of this erstwhile establishment?"

"By all means."

As he put a napkin into the page of the mystery book, he noticed there were other lines of poetry.

"Damian, do you realize what mysteries are in between the covers of this book?"

"Typographical? Clerical? Ghost stories?"

"No, no, my friend, someone has appealed to my Sherlockian intent only to serendipitously introduce us to poesy."

"Well, most of that is mysterious."

"You mean Blake, maybe, or Wordsworth?"

"Gentlemen, any decisions?"

"Ahh yes, the matter at hand."

"You know we close at 10."

"But it's only 7:30."

"Exactly."

"I'll take the special."

"What's that?"

"It's a local Dungeness crab served with an aioli sauce."

"Perfect."

Damian's eyes lifted themselves over the menu until he quietly said, "I'll take the fish and chips."

"Drinks?"

"Shall we get some local wine?"

"Of course, from the famous Napa Valley?"

"We have house wine."

"That's it?"

"All right, a house white it shall be."

They watched the waitress work the tables. They could see she was a pro and, if motion studies were done on her, she could probably teach most people something on the economy of movement. Every motion seemed to take into account two or three actions. She never walked anywhere without, either, getting an order or setting down an order. On one of her settings, she juggled two wine glasses, a bottle of wine, two salads, a glass of water and menus.

"Now, what do we call such a pro?" Schilling said loudly enough for her to hear.

"How about Rosa," the waitress answered.

"Ah, Rosa, the riveter."

"Wrong profession."

"Yes, of course, but you do have our riveted attention."

"Clever, where did you say you come from?"

"From the Midwest, young lady, but our names they mean nothing."

"You sound like a comedy routine."

"Hopefully, a compliment."

"Yea, you should go to the Community Center tonight. They have an open-mike. You guys would probably bring the house down."

"I've heard of earthquakes in this area."

"Verbal quakes, in this case."

"That's good, Rosa, verbal quakes. What say you Damian, shall we stroll over after our repast."

Before they could articulate any more, Rosa was already balancing their plates with a meatloaf special, which she gave to a rather colorful and loud-voiced man in the corner. He was wearing a Pendleton shirt with a black beret and noticeably drawing on the paper placemat with a red marker.

"Is he one of the local characters?" Damian asked her, as she placed the fish and chips and the evenings special on their table.

"He's one of the eccentrics all right but, actually, he's also an artist, emphasizing in, if you like, Grandma Moses."

"Please elaborate."

"He does naive pictures of San Francisco."

"Now, there's a combination."

"Naive pictures of a naive San Francisco?"

"What would Jack London say? "

"He was from Oakland."

"That's a good one!" The artist of a naive San Francisco had come over to their table and had spoken like a Greek stentorian for all to hear.

"So, you are the artist our waitress has expounded on," Schilling responded.

"I am not as naive as she likes to think. And it's not just because I disdain the quality of aesthetic recognition in this establishment."

This was all said in a voice that, perhaps, would get a reaction from someone in the restaurant but everyone seemed to ignore it accept Rosa who whirled back, " Grandma Moses has more going for her than you do, at least she's famous. "

"See what I have to put up with."

"May we perhaps see some of your work?"

"I only have a small canvas here but I am working on getting postcards made for the tourists, that is, as soon as I can interest someone in this potentially rewarding investment."

Looking at us with imploring eyes, he paused for a moment. When he heard or saw no response, he went on with his own putdowns of Rosa, the shop, even Bolinas, until another customer finally shouted, "That's enough, you damned curmudgeon, if you don't like it here, why don't you move."

"Heavens, I do like it here. Where else can I vent my spleen like this."?

Schilling and Damian looked at each other as if there were taking notes for their ongoing study of odd California fauna.

"It's been a pleasure," Schilling said and finally started to eat his *special*. Damian, too, began to eat, leaving the artist in limbo. Quietly, he retrieved a small canvas and placed it on their table. It was an intensely colored watercolor view of a cable car dropping down Hyde Street with two naked women standing on the car's platform while San Francisco

Bay and Alcatraz faded into the distance.

"The tourists like them," was faintly heard as he sat back down, apparently on his local perch.

"Now there's an oxymoron."

"Funny thing," Damian said quietly, "a local bohemian pandering to the tourists."

"Money is the root of all pandering," Schilling responded.

"Is that on the square root level," Damian asked, with an emphasis on the 'square'.

"Well, in this case 'square' can come from the *beat* era."

"And root can come in edible roots or country routes."

"And money still takes it all."

"Damian, are we so hip, so cool, that we can continue to abstract these issues or did we lose it somewhere? "

"Maybe we never had it."

"Maybe, maybe..." his voice getting serious, Schilling looked up and around the room and finally out of the window to see two colorful teenagers - one with a tie-dyed sunburst peeking out of an opened fur coat, his long hair wrapped under a knitted hat, the other wore dark glasses, a tuxedo jacket with tails, with a chartreuse scarf wrapped around him.

"There, Damian, goes our query - the not so elusive hippie. Are they a phenomenon of material excess or are they soul searchers or are they a cultural evolution or revolution or..." he caught himself and went back to his entree.

"We will have to work fast before they burn themselves out, " Damian added, but before he could go back to his fish and chips, the two rainbow regaled peacocks came into the shop and announced that there was a *happening* tonight. "It's a happening at the center, man, we're getting down, it's going down tonight...Be there,"

Be there! echoed around the room until the pandering artist told them to shut up and peddle their message elsewhere.

To Schilling it was all fodder for his dissertation. For Damian, there was the outward observance of the colorful scene as well as an inner response, which became a slightly unsettling convergence of interest and intrigue, affecting him on a deeper level. He could feel it but he could not verbalize it, not yet anyway, yet the words were there, somewhere in the world, somewhere in his mind, somewhere the words were forming...

This time Damian picked up the *mystery* book, flipped the pages and randomly stopped to read:

I can almost
   feel
the almost ancient
   feeling...
An upwelling of childhood memories
and more?
The soft radiant glow

of three candles
lit
on the Sunday of the third advent,
so much closer to the darkest day,
the longest night
of our yearly journey
around the life giving light
of the sun.
We have come so far
throughout each year
of meaning...
Now the candlelight sends its glow
it's radiance
it's beams
outward from within
Outward
to enlighten the space
where darkness dwells.
The choir sings
The long coffee table holds an offering
a Satsuma tangerine
the smooth wood of a piano gleams nearby
A music manuscript waits for life
the softness of a sheepskin languishes
On the couch with black pillows
I rest my worn out older body...
warmed by the continual flowing flames of the three candles
the light streams into me
and warms my long ago childhood
Emotions
and ancient remembrances
cherished and radiating
within the growing
Darkness...

11

Life-Cycles

"Darkness..." Damian repeated the word, and nodded with an inner affinity while Schilling looked at him in silence. In this moment of reverie, Damian's thoughts on his life flashed in front of him...Up until now, up until now, he thought, and even more, he felt, that he had lived a life living other people's expectations. He had gotten married at a young age, because, well, because, it turned out, she, his young first love, enticed him into the mysteries of her soft enclosing warmth. If it was destined to be, it was to be, he thought. Even earlier, however, from his early school years on, he had met the requirements of his teachers - all the way into the University. He had wanted to become an engineer, but instead, met the needs of an unexpected family. Now, close to 28 years old - the end of the fourth seven-year cycle of his short life - he was, for the first time, asking himself some very hard questions: What did he really value? What did he really want to pursue in his life. The luxury of his earlier youth was gnawing on him and the irony of these 28 years seemed to be that he thought he knew who he was.

Who told him of seven-year cycles anyway? He wasn't sure anymore.

Some called it biography and incorporated these seven year characteristics into human life cycles - the first seven were sense-oriented dependency; the next seven came with a change of teeth, mobility and physical awareness, the next seven brought about puberty and adjoining physical changes, the beginnings of individual awareness, separation from parents, the next seven – to age 21- brought about physical maturity and grown-up intellectual inquiry -going into the world; taking on jobs and a family, the next seven gave him enough years to look back on and see influences and patterns in his life, to see what he had learned. Did these timely temporal patterns really mean anything? He wasn't sure but it seemed to him that he had followed the script, these seven-year cycles, to some degree, but he could not understand why he did not stay with his dream of becoming an engineer; an inventor of structures. He grew up examining the world - as a child he had accumulated his own chemicals (largely from the kitchen cabinets - he could still remember combining bicarbonate of soda with Postum - horrendous). In addition, he had collections of bugs and stamps and coins of the world. He knew others, who had a more focused approach to the world. One of his many cousins, for example, had no qualms about getting what he wanted and would not have gotten married just because his girlfriend was pregnant, that is, if she did not fit into his plans. Somehow, he wasn't brought up like that, it just seemed obvious that he would be responsible for his actions, yet, it seemed like he had put his life on hold whenever he had responded, responsibly, to the situations he was involved in.

As a result he had felt enough frustrations building up in him to take some time off and go with his friend on this sojourn to California. He, too, would answer the call of the west, a hundred or so years after the forty-niners had staked their claims and some 400 years after the conquistadors had searched for El Dorado and the priests had searched for lost souls and who knows how many years after the Miwok had set up camps. There had been arguments and sadness after he did decide to go – his wife knew, then, that their relationship would not be the same if he took this journey - but his life had come to this point and his friend understood him, at least he thought he did. At this point Damian's eyes widened to take in his friend. It was just enough to wonder why he, Schilling, had come on this pilgrimage.

What were his reasons for coming here? Ostensibly, to do research for a doctorate in cultural anthropology, but his inner reasons were more complex or perplexing. For one thing his middle name was Homer and ever since he could remember he was a storyteller, as his namesake. He couldn't help it. His life was one story after another, Just as Odysseus traveled around a mythical Aegean to hear the stories of the living inhabitants who welcomed him, Schilling had traveled from his early youth - earlier than he'd like to remember- traveled from one foster home after another. In one, the man spoke with a German accent and told of the new world being born in Germany while his wife sang folk songs from the Arzt-Gebirge – this, Schilling remembered. In another home, he was less than their dog, begging for food, made to recite verses from the Old Testament before he could eat - *I will lift up mine eyes unto the lord...* that, he remembered. On another island, another home, his mother changed his name to Joseph, who had been lost for 12 years and now was back. They tried to get him to dance the Hora but his two left feet hindered him – this, he remembered.

Sometime, in his late teens, he met this vibrant, intense, wild-eyed, wavy-haired woman who bemusedly smiled at his awkward antics. Something must have resonated with them, however, because she wanted to take care of him and he wanted to be taken care of until...until he lashed out because he could not accept her *all consuming* love - he was not worthy - he was suffocating, until they made love and the house shook, but it would not last. His late 20s ended up with him divesting himself of everything except a zafu cushion on which he meditated and chanted for hours. After a few years of almost being there he decided to finish his studies. That was the state of this modern day Ulysses.

They had met each other at Vern's Bierstube - a local watering hole next to the campus. It was home to Joyce and Proust and Renoir and Bergman and Felini and countless others whose ideas were imbibed with strong beer. Among the layers of peanut shells they told each other their stories. Damian talked about a wall that had been built up until he could hardly see over it, Schilling talked of rebuilding a wall that had crumbled. From there they listened to each other until both had heard enough, until their friendships settled into an understanding and their circumstances evolved to a point where a trip together kept coming into the conversation...

Now, here they were in Bolinas with an invitation to go on a 'happening'. And it happened at the end of their meal at the Shoppe and after the book of mysteries had been closed. It happened when Damian, with eyes as wide as Malcolm McDowell in *A Clockwork Orange*, said, "Schilling, I don't think we should disappoint them, do you?"

"Damian, it is a necessary part of our research."

Slowly, without any warning, Ave Maria came into their awareness, from speakers throughout the restaurant, creating a mood of such beauty that they were seduced by it, closing their eyes and letting the tenor's voice take them out of their immediate surroundings, letting their minds wander back to the beach...Schilling let the music enshroud the innocence of the young girl they had seen, while trying to exorcize the inexplicable after effects of the howling apparition, Damian, however, reveled in the ethereal images of the evenings mist, his senses open...

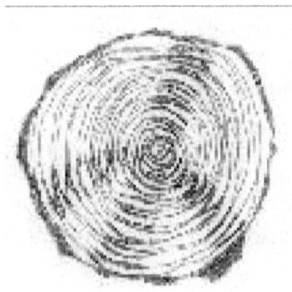

12

Happening

"Anything else tonight, dreamers?"

Startled by her insistence they both jerked up, "No, no, we're fine."

"Here's the damage."

After a customary analysis of all costs and the waitress' threat to have them put on the dread '86' list, there were finally back on the main street walking towards the Community Center. The night had filled with the aroma of the sea. They took deep breaths and let their eyes follow the mesa up and into the firmament, just in time to witness a shooting star.

"A momentary reminder of cosmic passion," Schilling articulated, as they looked into the semi darkness.

"Perhaps it's another omen," Damian added, "Maybe, this one will translate into something positive," as he thought back on the ethereal and eerie atmosphere on the beach. But, even now, the Mesa loomed darker over them, a view of solidarity and yet, also a reminder of fragility. As they walked down Main Street to the Community Center the air filled up with the sound of an acoustic guitar being strummed in a Calypso rhythm. It was a lone singer in front of the library, presumably not wanting to wait his turn at the open mike,

out of the west there came a man
rodi o diodi o di o
And in his Script there was a plan
rodi o diodi o di o...
"I hear the natives strumming."
"I presume the ritual has begun."
As if drawn to a flame, the two explorers wandered through an over growth of greenery, a canopy filled with small flowers that looked like Japanese lanterns lighting their way, until they came to an almost closed door where the nasal sounds of another singer's voice could be heard,
my love she sleeps like silence
They pushed the door inward, which widened the sliver of light,
without ideals or violence
she doesn't have to say she's faithful
yet she's true
like ice, like fire...
They could barely make out the outline of a tall longhaired singer through a light-filled haze, wafting through a rainbow sea of colors. The haze smelled sweet and the spotlight occasionally illuminated a plethora of turquoise or magenta or a golden yellow or even the calm in-between color of fringed buckskin. Everyone seemed to be listening intently. It was not what they had expected. They allowed themselves a slow entrance to the poetry of the songwriter and of the singer who, by now, had several local musicians backing him up including Surfer. When it ended, the rainbow crowd whooped and hollered and clapped for more.
"...that, of course, was a song written by Dylan, Bob Dylan, in case anyone didn't know. Now, I thought, maybe I could add one of my own. Something that has been nagging me, something I've been wondering about...he turned to the musicians and said, "It's in D, if you want to join me..."
He plucked one string after another and closed his eyes, remembering the words and the night he forged them,
As I look outside my window
And see the garden growing green
It's hard to think of this all passing
Like the remnants of a dream...
Where is the voice that speaks for truth?
Where is the voice that speaks for all?
Is it just a twilight shadow?
No more than writing on the wall
Inside the minds of desperation
Is a threat to all we know
I'd like to think it's an illusion
But they build to bring our fall
Where is the voice that speaks for love?
Where is the voice that speaks for all?
Is it just a twilight shadow?

No more than writing on the wall

The arpeggios continued as Surfer added an emphasis with his bass while the ethereal flowing of sounds from a nearby flute let the melody float on the hazy air. Shiva let it continue until the time was right to continue…

As I stand beside the river
And hear the ancient water flow
It seems as though I'm moving
And change is all I know
Where is the voice that speaks for truth?
Where is the voice that speaks for all?
Is it just a twilight shadow?
No more than writing on the wall
No more than writing on the wall
No more than writing on the wall
No more than writing on the wall

His voice dissolved into a sighing breath while the vibrations of the guitar strings died down and the musician's accompaniment quieted down and the writing on the wall finally faded out. It was then that Shiva looked into the audience and asked them to ponder another question, "This is also one I've thought about. What are we doing here?" He let a silent response continue and changed the question, "I'll put it another way, what are we changing here?"

After what seemed a long moment of anticipation someone in the smoky, hazy crowd shouted out,

"the world, man."

"yea!"

"the wheels of oppression."

"Yea, yea…"

"And what about those?" he shot back.

"Faceless bureaucrats." came from one corner.

"The machine!" came from another corner, until shouting phrases and words bounced all around the auditorium.

"What kind of machines?"

"Killing machines!"

"Yea, right on…"

"And what are we changing here?" he shouted louder, to be heard again. Only this time the strings of his guitar vibrated with the final word and continued with the repeated phrase that echoed back, "What are we changing here, " until the audience was with him, chanting with him, "What are we changing here?"

Between the chanted phrases he called out, "Everything we can!"

"What are we changing here?" the rainbow crowd shouted back.

"Everything we can, everything that's wrong that needs to be changed, everything artificial, everything that's worshipped and paid for by someone else's sweat and tears bound by someone else's greed…"

"What are we changing here?" they asked again.

"Everything we can, everything that makes us less than what we are, what we can be, what we can see, what we can do, I'm talking to all of us, I'm talking to all of you, it's not enough to just sit back and let someone bring us down into the ground and grind us down into what they want us to be..."

"What are we changing here?" they wanted more,

"Everything we can, everything that makes us live less than what we are what we can be..."

"What are we changing here?"

The phrase kept repeating, inducing, repeating, transforming in the hazy smoky sounding night until even Schilling and Damian could no longer keep an objective distance in the midst of the chanting moving charging bodies...They began to feel something else stir in this communal revelry of faces voices spewing words in an abandon of past and future, they were here, in the now and Shiva was leading them...

"What are we changing here?"

Who knew what was what except to be here now was stealing this moment from the balls and chains of the past, "Be here now!" they heard him say between the chanting phrases, "Be here now!" While conga drums echoed the words...

And they were here! Now! Until some kids actually dropped from exhaustion, falling on the hard wood floor while guitars joined in and congas beat the phrases in pounding rhythm...

"Schilling!" Damian shouted but it was too late, there was no more retreat from the moment, the 'happening' the haze, the smoke, the beat, the sounds, the *happening* that was changing the world, here, in this outpost on the coast of California around an ever changing lagoon and the shifting sands of a wood-strewn beach and a falling mesa and the violet hills of the princess over looking her thousand year-old rituals, something indeed was happening coalescing into the chanting realms of "What are we changing here?" interspersed with "Everything we can!"

"What are we changing here?"

"Everything we can!"

"What are we changing here?"

"Everything we can!"

"What are we changing here?"

Their call and response call and response became quieter, moonlight was setting over the fields, and it was time to go home. Shiva's voice, almost inaudible, ended with:

Be

Here

Now!

13

Kiss

Damian had fallen into the bodies filling the floor, lost to all but the warmth of their breathing. It had all become a blur as if he had dropped into the poetry of Novalis, Rumi or the sensuous writings of Anais Nin. He had become a virtual, fictional, unreal character yet, seemingly, so real, so filled with sensory openness; drawing in the moment... yes, he was here...now, yes, his head was swimming, he did not want this to end...and it did not end, it was just the beginning...

At the feet of Shiva the singer were glazed-over budding blossoming flower children strewn about the floor, on pillows, off pillows, wherever their bodies wound down - clothed in all their finery - embroidered vests over Russian shirts with full sleeves, yards of gunny-sack skirts, loose cotton shirts over the budding nipples of girls with inviting eyes...A roach was passed around and around with the sound of a late-night rock duo singing in the background *buh dah da da dah feelen groovy...feelin groovy*...wafting within and without the hazy smoky air...Damian gazed around in soft wonder until the eyes of the girl next to him caught his, they smiled slightly and knowingly, she opened her mouth, as if to speak, as if to speak...and she spoke silently with her mouth and her eyes until he slowly leaned over, closer, closer until he brought his lips close to hers, closer, closer, it was magnetic electric, there were sparks, he could feel them, he could...he touched her lips, he felt her lips, soft, drawing him into a world he did not know existed... ultimately, in the moment, he did not care if it ever ended, if he ever woke up...if he ever...such was his state of bliss...a reasoning mind overwhelmed by his senses, wallowing and wandering into a timelessness inextricably intertwined with his emotions. He had touched a time and place that was inside him, bound in his memory, which just needed an opening, a portal to go through – Dali, Magritte and the surrealists had painted it for him – a melting clock, a face of sky surrounded by trees. A portal that let him float above a swelter of bodies melting around him, someone had initiated him with a kiss and took him into a time and place of his own remembrance; a corner of the world, where things were as they could be, where he sat with a good cup of coffee next to him, steaming on the table covered with an old table cloth while the rain beat down on the alley outside. It's Christmas time and the sidewalk glistened, reflecting the pulsating white lights put up on the trees by the proprietor of a bohemian cafe, lining a sidewalk slice of the city...the sounds of Amazing Grace, in an unknown language, coming from some unknown source and exquisitely sung until every word was felt, until he was no longer lost or blind but could see and feel the grace of life, be alive, with a momentary feeling of gratitude welling up that he wished would continue...Is that so hard? To continue this feeling? Now, a melody is played by a balalaika, it begins slowly, arcs upward and, as if hanging by a star, while he is holding his breath, it comes back down to the glistening snow...every moment went deeper into all he knew, all he had experienced...He had rarely felt such gratefulness. His tears came, overwhelming him, from the depths of what he had stored away, waiting for someone to awaken the memories – is it possible that every once in a while someone opens the door to these storerooms; that in a particular moment, someone can come in to rummage around and resurrect the collective cultural icons, the sounds words voices images smells, from the depths of our personal memory and collective consciousness...yes Jung yes symbols yes hidden deep in the collective unconscious...

Did he still believe that? - Odette Dylan Simon Cohen Bret Baez Lennon Hesse...the magic theater...Lara's theme...Lara...La...his mind going at breakneck speed with images and icons plopping up and down like the mud pots in Yellowstone Park, fed by superheated underground water... until...until the landscape changed, and he, again, became aware of his fragile place in the world. *How do we know what is passed on to the future?* He silently cried out, *do we know if symbols, icons, snippets of melody, or an emotional meeting of mouths are passed on? Can it be that all meaning, all beauty, all meaning of beauty and love are created by us and will one day be gone...?*

No! Do not think like that; try to simply remember that this precious time,

64

these few moments of flesh, amidst the terror of the cosmos and our own self-made horrors, these few short moments of joy on a small blue sphere are all we have...
Can it be!
*No! I cannot live with the thought of it all being a meaningless moment of biological life, yet, yet we I we I squander the very time we have. On what? As if to wait for death, as if we were immortal. Maybe our DNA has already programmed the desire for death; has already encoded the wish for death in it so that we do not want to live longer! Or else we would go mad with the awareness of our short moment in the midst of nothingness...*And I read my Sherlock Holmes and you play your moonlight waltz and I do my crossword puzzle and you play your scrabble game and I have my glass of wine and you drive from here to there...thinking that you're needed, feeling that you're needed, creating the needs to be needed... while you feel the pangs of hunger and the fear of frost. And I carry my address book for the call that must be made because the connection must continue even in the sound of silence and I want to keep on doing and you want to keep on doing because the mirror is behind us because the mirror is behind us and nothing is reflected and we're afraid to turnaround afraid to face the nothing... afraid to turn around because the mirror has no image...

14

Beginning

Finally, finally, please, back to the now of the smoky room, Damian rationalized and returned and looked around, dazzled by the colors, remembering the soft wonder of the girl next to him...She was still here, after their moment of melting mouths...

On the stage, a makeshift stage, under the basketball halo hoop of a different kind, Shiva was overcome with the incessant euphoric ecstatic chanting. Exhausted and spent, he had sat down on a chair someone had built for this makeshift stage, which added to this moment of suspended belief. It was fit for royalty. With a glow about him, he was reflected in the bobs and baubles and sequins glued onto this uniquely created oneofakind chair - a three-dimensional collage of mirrors...he had sunk into it, his body was limp and yet the glow of his being showed through and reflected outwardly from the mirrors giving those who looked upon him, the feeling of an almost sensory transcendent experience. Silence was beginning to flood the hall and taking over again. The air was left with the light flowing between him and the rapturous few remaining in the hall. Some had left for the cool night air, as had Schilling. The scene had been too much for him; his need for objective distance had broken the spell woven in the music and the smoke. He had left Damian, flayed, open to his senses. At the same time, he was or, he felt, this touch of apprehension, a vague yet almost fearful apprehension, like a teenager after his first sexual experience…he had been allowed to witness a final act of innocence and experience the first act of knowledge…the world had changed, from here on they would not be the same, this was Schilling's apprehension, something had happened here that could not and would not go back to where it had been…He walked in a daze back to Smileys, grateful for the cool night air. Damian would have to make it back on his own.

And Damian did make it back, late in the night, or early in the morning, rapping on the door, no key in his pocket, waiting for Schilling to wake up and let him in. It was then that he noticed the morning glow behind the breasts of the princess. How subtle, he thought, how gentle the spectrum of light is that transforms the night into a new morning. He did not even hear the unlocking of the lock but turned the knob finding the door ready to open. With a push, the light caressed Schilling, who had gone back to his bed. Damian closed the door, fell into the other double bed and died to the waking world…letting the night melt into his past.

Something had happened. It was not easy to say what – was it a convergence of cosmic events meeting the earth, or a consciousness of enough human beings causing a critical mass of understanding? Was this a collective recognition of the senses, charged with music grass rainbow colors, acid...Did I said acid? Yes, acid, the mind bending wending intensing rending sending lending feeling state of being...somehow once upon a time we did not mind meeting Donald Duck on blotter paper. No, let me go...when will it end? end...end...I don't know. This, this is the beginning of the new age...

15

Voices

After his transcending trip to the moon, Shiva made his way back to the House of Aquarius, the heartfelt hotel, the Grandiose Hotel. Sweet held him, half dragged him, along with several other intoxicated revelers, back to the room, put him on the big bed and let him sink into it. His mind was soon in a dream world of his own recollections, connecting his momentary state with past images, moving, focusing…until a knight's banner was seen hanging from the ceiling of the Museum Café - a blue cross on a white background. Who left it there? How many years ago? A longhaired crusader? A street corner singer who went by the initials of SC, who was now calling himself Shiva – the lord of the dance? Did he leave it there, on his way to his destined call, just around the corner, in a turn of the road? Where, once upon his quest, he had a chance encounter with Jack, the poet, who had talked to him of poetry and songs and when SC, within the conversation, questioned the worth of a poem, Jack stated, in an incredulous voice, "If you have to ask, then you haven't been called." This struck him, as if pierced by the harpoon displayed on the wall. He wasn't sure how to respond, he had to convince Jack and himself that this was in him, almost, in desperation, he pulled out a crumpled sheet of paper with coffee stained writing on it and read it to him:

If you should question
The reason you write
The worth of your words
On a solitary night
As you sit by the candle
And the stained coffee cup
Remember dear poet
You're not the first to have
Hungered and thirsted for a word
That would answer the needs of the times
That would answer the needs of your mind
In your moment of fear
When you straddle the edges so deep
That you know
So dark
That you know
So deep and so dark
That you cry out to one
Who will answer you now now now now
Listen
To the movement of the night
A million circles still in flight
They will bring you back in sight
Listen
And
Be still...

"We are the voices that silence has anointed..." was all that Shiva heard before he went into a deep sleep.

16

Revelations

A palpable buzz could still be felt in the community after the now famous *happening*. It was still being talked about, not only on Main Street and both mesas, but also throughout the farthest reaches of Marin County. It was not necessarily the world, but the excitement definitely reflected what was in the general consciousness. Word spread via hitchhikers and low wattage radio stations sending out a deejays banter along with every local rock folk psychedelic band that had enough money to send in a demo. Something was definitely going on, coming down, breaking in, even Schilling had started to write his voyeuristic experiences in his personal journal which added to his copious notes from his field experiences. Damian had ritually broken his pencils, broken them and thrown them into a fire that several colorful revelers had built on the beach, all the while chanting *the map is not the territory, the map is not the territory* until all in between media, all contrivances that had kept him from immediate experience were put on the altar - *the map is not the territory*...Was he playing at this? Was it a hollow gesture? A symbolic act caught in an impetuous moment?

"I can afford to break a few pencils," he thought, "What would it cost? I can write about it later, no justification needed…"

The beach had come alive with revved up energy. Hippies were anointed with a new calling. Hollywood roamed about the beach drumming, giving the post *happening* days a heart beat…adding to the chanting dancing music coming out of any small gathering at any odd and feel-good time - there was no hesitation…

The Grandiose Hotel also had its share of visitors, many gathering in the kitchen, with herbal tea brewing, the alluring smell of Constant Chai and the sweet aroma of local grass. Communion was in the air, with the expectant wondering when the newly ordained guru would come down - the word had spread of this Bard of Bolinas, this Invoker of Ecstatic States. They milled about the small kitchen; occasionally going into the second-hand store to buy whatever wild and strange vintage piece of clothing Val had accumulated in his estate gatherings. There were nobeatnoheatnodeep books left and as soon as bootleg recordings came into the pile of contemporary sounds they were gone…There was no hurry, there was only possibility…Shiva had stayed in his room the last several days - if someone was counting - he was furiously writing down new thoughts, new lyrics - words of wisdom…words of love…words that would take them all into the new age…

I'm telling you now
Well, you're lifetime goes so fast
Times are on the run
Listen to me, friend
Don't you see?
What could be done?
Don't be a fool
Don't be a fool
Just
Jump into the ocean
Jump in while you can
Jump into the ocean
Jump in while you can
The hours of indecision only wear away your plans
And then you're torn
by late night questions
And you'll drown in late night tears
And you will see your past before you
And you will wail against the sky
crying for redemption
Trying not to lie iiiiiii
Knowing no one hears you
Hoping someone might
Knowing no one hears you
Hoping someone might
He repeated the phrase softer now,

Hoping someone might
But he did not really, could not really, instead he wrote words of doing...
So I'll tell you again
If you think you're life's undone
And you write your ages down
Listen to me friend
Don't you see?
What could be done?
Don't be a fool
Don't be a fool
Just
Climb the highest mountain
Climb it while you can
Climb the nearest mountain
Climb it while you can
The hours of convenience
Are lost upon the sand
And then you're torn
By late night questions
And then you'll drown
In late night tears
And you'll see your past before you
And you will wail against the sky
Crying for redemption
Trying not to lie
Knowing no one hears you
Hoping someone might
Knowing no one hears you
Hoping someone might
So I'm telling you now
Our life times go so fast
Times are on the run
Listen to me, friend
Listen to me, friend...
Listen...

17

Firework

He mouthed the word over and over again…listen, listen, listen…taking in and letting out the meaning of both; listening to the silence and to the speaking, while they were waiting for him, listening for his words…Sweet was with him, as was Surfer and a bearded man named Marshall, who had come into the fold. The commotion in the kitchen reverberated up the stairs and the herbal fragrances oozed under their door. They knew or felt something, only Shiva attempted to stay and work through it…until the evening's empire was suspended by a loud light-filled blast outside their window - a July 4th star-filled firework had been set off not too far from the hotel, its shower of firecracker mini blasts of light set the crowd off in a response of 'wow' and 'yeaaaaaaa'. Shiva had looked in the direction of the window, the portal of his earlier inner revelations, just as the burst and blast of a hundred fire red stars filled it's transparent opening. He went to it, hoping to keep the star moment alive but its beauty and effect were momentary. Looking out, he tried to keep the lights from fading and screwed the windows open breathing in the powdered air. Someone shouted, "Shiva" but he did not hear them, he was still looking through the looking glass seeing reflections imbued with the red glow, seeing two roads, one of them evoking a man with a burden on his shoulder, carrying a makeshift frame of wood that seemed much too heavy for him, with an old man sitting in the frame fondling, what looked like, prayer beads, and chanting in a low voice, over and over, the sound of *Om mani padme hum*...Over and over the sound resounded in the stark barren mountain valley. He could see the carrier, struggling with determined steps, continuing over the holy and rocky ground. He felt the weight of the old man, not overwhelming, but ongoing, constant. His continued chanting set the tempo of the young man's walk...*om mani padme hum*...His steps, when possible, had taken on the inner beat of the rhythmic chanting. They walked together, yet, where were they going? The question out of the mountainous past seemed to echo around them. The sage fondled the beads hoping to quell the outer-inner sound, their touch stimulated his fingers, yet the sound continued, grew louder and echoed through out the night...*where are you going?* It resounded. *Where are you going.........?*

With his ears poised to the echo of that eternal question and his eyes intensely gazing into the pane, Shiva was trying to make sense of the image, until, reluctantly yet inevitably, he saw himself carrying the frame on his back, with the holy man in it. Hardly any words were spoken, only the rhythmic steps of his leather clad feet on the worn down rock of the age-old path. In the cadence of his steps he wondered how many worn and weary pilgrims had walked over this hard rock on their way to nirvana, as they were striving for enlightenment, searching for meaning or, or the letting go of searching? Is that possible? Can one? Anyone? Let go of searching? And do what? Live? How? These ancient pilgrims had put one foot in front of the other carrying carrying carrying...until the path hardened and the expanse around him widened into a barren rock strewn valley, surrounding mountains broke the sky with their crags and peaks, impaling the clouds...He walked with determination, his back laden with the wooden frame, large enough to hold the old Scraggly bearded man who had somehow conformed to the shape of the apparatus.

Had he taken this on or was he born with it, this burden of striving for another world? His parents had been born into a religion and, now, here, he was in the midst of a struggle to find a religion, or a spiritual calling and...to endure hardship as part of this sacred calling. "The greater the struggle," he thought, "the more blessed he would be in the next life, within 'the gates of Eden' - back with his creator..." For most of his young life he did not have to look for hardship, his father had been out of work for years, it was the time of ruinous economic and social disasters. Inflation had destroyed the basic currency. People filled wheelbarrows with worthless money to buy a loaf of bread. What government assistance they got went to pay for the room the family lived in - the parents and three children in one room with a toilet down the hall. Fortunately they had a small garden plot on the outskirts of town where they grew a few vegetables. Yet, out of these conditions he harbored no bitterness, just the opposite, he held a firm belief that this was a test, that he had been sent here to see how he would respond to these hardships. With much ingenuity he spent time, as a boy, around street gratings, getting the coins out that someone had accidentally dropped in. He put old gum on a stick and poked it down in between the bars to nab a coin. It was better than fishing, which he also did through the ice in the winter, because it was the only money he ever put in his pocket. As a teenager, he studied the Scriptures - the Bible and the Book of Mormon - and talked to people about the savior. Often he would be so hungry that when he had a slice of bread and only one piece of thin salami he would slide the salami off the bread pretending to have eaten it. This way he had two salami sandwiches. Yet, when the time came for him to leave the household, he was as strong as a young man could be, physically and spiritually. He had a fervent belief combined with an intellectual curiosity...and he could walk. He could carry his belief on strong legs with rhythmic footsteps throughout that 'lonesome valley', singing a song that he resonated with, a song he knew well and carried with a wavering voice. Yes, he was on a spiritual pilgrimage with the clear eyes of someone seeing beyond the desolate rocks, with the heartfelt emotion of someone who could walk forever...he carried the old wizened chanting praying pilgrim on his back...

Om mani padme hum om mani padme hum grew quieter and fainter as the barren slate of the ancient mountains turned, turned into the other side of his mind, his inner struggle turned into the cement pillars of a grand arena defined by shafts of light shooting into the sky. It was a rally for a demigod.

Where are you going? Where...are...you...going...?

The question still echoed in the cement filled plaza. But it did not bother the man, Shiva saw, emerging from a bunker like cavern, a man with a determined gaze mounting a podium and looking into 10,000 faces, waiting in eagerness, waiting for his every word...10,000 uniformed men waiting in anticipation. The air was charged with something intangible, something rising out of their collective desires, something greater than each one of them.

As he straightened his jacket and gave himself a discerning look in the mirror he felt a stirring throughout his body, an emotional intensity that overwhelmed his routine awareness of who he was and, more important, who he could be; who he was destined to be. He looked again and felt the need to be acknowledged, to feed this inner intensity...He needed to be recognized.

With a single-mindedness he had left the waiting room and joined his advisors and his generals to walk the long walk in front of the thousands of eager straining faces, the air was alive with their desperation. For what? For salvation? In slow cadence they walked through the uniformed men, eyes blazing from within, meeting each gaze, their hearts pounding, their metal gleaming with quick bursts of light, reflecting off their helmets and steel rifles and medals...This was his realm. He had prepared himself for this. This was his destiny. He would bring them to the greatness they deserved...someone, out of the thousands, somewhere in the thousands, someone shouted: "Caesar". A lone voice answered back, "Hail Caesar". The flood gate opened to one after another, "Hail Caesar, Hail Hail Heil   Hail Hail Heil Heil Caesar...The tumult rose, careening through the multitude, rolling under his feet, lifting him up on their exhortations until he could be seen by every eye and he could hear every mouth embody him in their hopes and dreams...Somehow he hovered over them, larger than life between the shafts of light. He knew this was his time, his moment. He knew what they wanted to hear. He had learned his lines well. With one hand slowly rising toward and over the crowd, the mass, the one, they began to quiet down until the silence of anticipation overcame them, until his arm was raised to the heavens, casting a shadow, a small one at first, a shadow that grew as he was to begin his oration to the glory of their spirit...

Men and women of this great nation I stand before you and celebrate your great achievements. You have risen to the highest of what it means to be human. Out of the forests of history you have grasped the possibilities that the gods of old had preordained for a people. Out of countless battles the strongest survived and you are the legacy of the strongest...

At this point a great yell of yes swept through the ranks, yes yes yes...

In this strength and through your intelligence you have achieved industrial and artistic miracles that are unprecedented in the history of humanity...

Yes yes yes...

With your will...your intelligence...your work...you will achieve even greater glory...

His voice was rising in an emotional crescendo rifle butts began pounding the pavement in rhythm...10,000 voices sounded as one...yes yes yes yes yes yes...

We stand as one people...one nation...one lea

BWANG BLANG BANG rang out rang out of nowhere out of no where no one expected shots rang out of somewhere someone had come out of nowhere, in slo mo, in front of all the high ranking medaled men, the five star generals, the 10,000 uniformed men and the followers of this demigod, who by now was sinking, the pristine Prussian blue cloth turning red oozing through the finely tailored cloth he was sinking down hanging onto the dais desperately hanging on, he was invincible, hanging on but the blood kept flowing out down his pants, onto the stage, onto the tarmac, into the 10,000, oozing into all until all melted into the blood red blood...

Damned world

The moment is lost

The life preservers have been tossed

And all the ship wrecked wrenching sailors

Will have a glimpse of the cross
You've grabbed what you could
With your fingers in knots
While the wind Scatters your secrets
To the ends of the earth
It's too late for a reprieve
It's too late…

Like lava from a never ending earthly source the oozing blood slowly congealed, turning shades of grey, transforming into a hard granite landscape with a worn over path and a familiar figure kneeling at a stopping point. He had just taken the scaffolding off his shoulders. The wizened hunched up holy man had gotten out and given him the prayer beads – they were for him. He rolled them over his finger tips, felt them and faintly heard an inner voice:

Alive you are everything…
Dead you is memory…

Alive you are everything…
Dead you is memory

18

What are we going to change?

"Shiva!" someone shouted, out of the darkness of the street. He turned and blinked his eyes toward the sound. Just as suddenly, the shafts of light that had framed the demigod's rally to future glory became a streetlight on the corner. He moved the windows, wondering where he had been.

"Sweet." he barely uttered her name.

She, too, had heard the call of his name, had seen him trancelike in front of the glass with strange patterns, had been waiting for him to come back...

"Sweet," he said again, "I have news from the interior of the world."

By now she had begun to take notes when he spoke.

"I'm listening," she said, as she grabbed her pencil and a notebook that she had entitled: *What we are going to change?*

"We must disregard fears, the fears of the unknown. They can grow inside us. They are inside us just as surely as they seem to come from outside us. In order to live with them we must live as if we had already died. Then each act would be free of fear. This is the faith of the fulfilled human being. From this awareness we can live in the moment, whether it is sowing a seed or washing a dish or making love or practicing the violin, each moment can become Pachelbel's *Canon in D* or an *Ode to Joy*, practiced and played a hundred times and yet each time played anew, the moment when a glimmer of light is refracted through a hand blown ruby red vase or the flutter of birch leaves dancing in the cooling breeze above a mountain lake or..."

While he was talking, Marshall entered the room to tell him of the crowds wanting to see him, wanting to get a glimpse of him...He wanted to tell him how many fans he had made, but, instead, he heard him speaking and silently sat down on the bed...Oblivious to the squeaky bedspring, as Shiva continued,

"I have seen a man search for enlightenment only to have the answer echo off hard granite walls, misinterpreted or denied...

I have seen the grasping for ultimate power only to see it die a million hellish deaths...and yet those who lived were still capable of tenderness to a child and kind to someone in need...

I have also seen us withdraw from touch to embrace the idea of touch...

I have experienced physical union...tantric union...its state of bliss...its moment of ecstasy...

So I say,

Let ecstasy enter your life..."

There was stillness after he said *life*. He turned around to look at Sweet and Surfer and Marshall and Jane Caravan, a frizzy-haired woman who had been beguiled by his ideas. Several others had also entered the open door of the west facing room. Among them was Damian with the young woman, (his latest endearment) and Mariah. Marshall was the first to speak, "Shiva, you're talking like a hermit who has gone to the mountain and looked down on our daily, sometimes petty, lives..."

He just smiled, "I've been to the top of Mount Tam and I've seen the great Pacific and touched the sky as it rolled over me. Have you felt that lately? It can be an ecstatic moment."

Sweet joined in, "We were overlooking Stinson Beach when we had that happen to us, and it was, like...like...it was like..." she wasn't sure how to end it, the image of Julia clouded her thoughts, she let the words float around them until they were all waiting, finally, with a questioning shaky voice she said, "wow..."

They let her perceived enthusiasm trail off until Marshall spoke again, "Look Shiva, I want to believe in what you're saying...but I need something..."

"What is your name?"

"Marshall."

"Do you believe in yourself?" Shiva's voice rose as he walked over to him.

"Yea, yes, sure..."

"And what do you believe in, Marshall, that you have lived to the fullest; that you have touched ecstasy in your moment of living?"

The encounter had focused all attention on Marshall, the wavering, and Shiva, the potential, until their dynamic intensity spread throughout the room. Shiva went on, at the same time capping both his hands on Marshall's cheeks, looking straight into his eyes, "Believe in your possibility, believe in your ecstasy, Marshall, believe in the moment!" He pulled Marshall's face close and kissed him on the forehead, pulled him closer and held him until there was nothing else in existence except their embrace...after an eternity, they moved apart, the air had changed, the mood was transcendent...Someone said 'he is enlightened', someone whispered, 'master'; someone said, 'he is the dharma', until almost everyone present in that room repeated his name...Shiva, Shiva, Shiva...

He went to one after the other and kissed them and embraced them until they all found a place to sit, against pillows and walls, on the two beds, while he sat on an old velvet cushioned chair near the window, an adjustable lamp showered him with just enough light to let his long hair glow. Caravan had brought her prayer rug and set up several brass bowls, the rims of which she began to circulate with a special stick, until an eerie whining sound emerged. She breathed on it and the air shifted, moving like waves into our ears, as if her breathing touched us...sending us all into an open state of receptivity, a mood in which Shiva ruminated and contemplated -

This had been his dream, a dream, that he thought, would not translate into actual reality. Still, he was reluctant to take it on and when it became a possibility, something inside him woke from its slumber. A deep age-old yearning grew in him as the events presented themselves, as he resonated with the inner longing of the many people who had heard him. Out of this, his voice had grown as well as his gestures. Just as the quiver of a leg to the beat of shake rattle and roll caused hysteric screaming, Shiva's slowly raised hands, in front of the anxious expectant followers, with three fingers outstretched and his thumb touching his little finger, caused them to grow quieter, until a reverence pervaded the distance between them...only then, with his right hand still signifying the triangle, the trinity, and his left hand loosely clutched in a ball, the circle of the infinite, only then, did he begin to speak with resonant tones,

"No matter how incredible individual creativity is, even, if, momentarily affecting many people, the work passes and they pass into the longer momentum of the ongoing world..."

For some it was not so much the meaning of the words but the sound of his voice that lulled them into his enlightened state, for others it was the ideas in the words, they sat with open faces; their eyes deep, like wells going into the reservoir of past needs and desires.

"Every creative work is a visible devastation of the turbulent overthrow of what is into what is possible from what was into what will be. The wheel of destruction and rebirth is as old as our memories enclosed in the blueprint of life..."

"For every moment of individual contemplation there are many people who keep the Scaffolding of the means of survival bolted together - whether it is picking lettuce, or collecting garbage at 4 in the morning..."

One after the other short spoken cultural comments or epistles as Jane had named them, brought about a quiet, barely audible response of "oh yea," and "Amen," and "wow"...

"Every attempt at explaining an after life comes down to the hope for immortality...the variety of explanations is a ten thousand year-old history of the realization and the consciousness of mortality. The belief of an ongoing individuality or soul is the supreme ego trip of human beings...the loss of loved ones is a loss inside ourselves, not the loss of the deceased...it is up to us to turn this loss into a recognition of having lived, having a chance to have lived with them - a child, a father, a friend - instead of a loss, it is a celebration..."

"The momentum of earthly history and the millions of people now making history is an accumulation of individual desires and needs for survival and all the levels and layers of human endeavors that are above and intertwined with human survival...and human survival is intertwined with all life sustaining life on the earth..."

"Every culture has evolved through and with the needs of survival; every individual familyclantribe has created customsritualsmeanings to perpetuate their hopes for survival and to lessen their fears of the unknown...he paused, as if to feel for the thread that connected his thoughts, percolating from some inner source, in his pause, the mood was receptive, the silence palpable, it was the sound of one hand clapping until he, literally, *clapped*, a ringing wake up call, for anyone who had fallen asleep...with wide-eyed listening around the room, he continued,

"The cultural constraints in the familyclantribe have become rules and regulations and eventually laws and constitutions in the so-called modern world...but the will of the people expressing itself in the on-going dance of life on this planet can and will bring change, in spite of the hanging on of certitude, comfort and security..."

"Out of individuals, such as yourselves, a dervish dance can begin, which can influence others and sometimes a critical mass can occur which can change the dominant paradigms of a community and a society and a cultural..."

"Let the dervish dance begin...let ecstasy become the new paradigm..."

As one after the other of his wide ranging cultural insights were spoken and cast out over the sea of listeners, as one after the other of the responses of "oh yea," and "far out," and "wow," had been heard again and again, there was, only slightly at first, a beginning, a murmur that started growing louder, wanting to respond, wanting to punctuate his voice, until, his words, his voice, his being, urged them to begin the dance...at some point someone stood up in a rapturous state moving and singing, over and over, *hall le lu yah hall lay lu yea yea yea* and swaying to the front, to be with him, to be near him, hall le lu yah hall le lu yea yea yea…as if driven by ancient rituals smoldering in their being…to be with him…

19

Reality Tonic

"I tell you, I sat listening to those bowls, Schilling," they vibrated through me. I almost felt like I was back on the beach, we were all on the same wavelength..."

Damian's voice grew more animated as he was telling him what had happened the previous night, the night in the west-facing room with the window of revelations. "Shiva came out of this trance with, or maybe he was still in a trance, with these, what he called insights, just rattled them off, at some point there was an encounter with this man named Marshall. He had been questioning Shiva on other occasions, only this time Shiva looked him in the eyes, asked him what he was searching for and finally embrace him. It changed the mood of the room. Out of it came this awareness of the moment. It's not a new idea, I know, but it was incredible to actually experience a kind of *being there* when everything else falls away and you're totally there...I've got to tell you that was not the first time, remember the night of the happening, the night you left early...next to me was this girl who looked like the girl we had seen on the beach, I was intoxicated, every girl looked like the girl on the beach, I'm not sure, but I saw her as the archetype of female receptivity. I was gone, Schilling, as some of these kids would say. I looked at her at one point and she looked at me and opened her mouth until I leaned close to her open lips to kiss her. It was so intense, it was electrical before we ever touched, I must say, it was a kiss that opened me up...she met me at the Grandiose. We were there, we were floating on those sounds. It seemed like the mood lasted...I didn't want it to end. I don't know when I left that room or when I came back here. What day is it?"

"Damian, I think you need a shot of hard stuff at Smileys, particularly with that biker, he'll add the reality tonic."

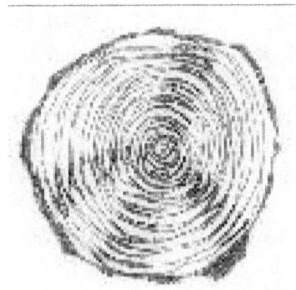

20

Stanford

A few days after the encounter at the Grandiose Hotel, a car pulled up to the Shoppe. It had a Stanford sticker on the rear window. Out of it came a preppy looking young man in a green corduroy jacket over a black turtleneck. He took a slow look around Main Street, sighed, and walked into the Shoppe. Inside, he saw a woman behind the counter. It was Sherry, the owner, who spent much of her day keeping some semblance of order in the restaurant. Unlike Mariah, who ran Scowleys out of her emotions and a sense of drama, Sherry was business, albeit, good-natured business and she had become a welcoming fixture for many a local. He walked up to her and pulled out a photograph, "Excuse me, but have you seen this woman?" he inquired in a matter of fact voice. It was a photo of a woman in a light tan jacket with a finely patterned gold and brown scarf loosely draped around her shoulders, a woman in her mid twenties with short brown hair. "She was heading this way a few weeks ago. I found her car near the Mount Tam highway. She hasn't called or been seen since..."

Sherry looked at the photo carefully. "I don't recall her, but then I've seen a lot of young women these last few weeks. Maybe Rosie or Josh has seen her. They come in around four for the dinner shift."

"I could check back. I'm probably going to stay the night."

"Smileys, across the street, has rooms."

"Thanks, I'll check back."

As the door to the Shoppe was closing behind him, someone jostled past him, knocking the photo out of his hand. For a moment he thought about leaving it on the cracked sidewalk. He hesitated, wondering if he should let her go, but in that moment, she came back to him. He still felt the pain of her words left under her cereal bowl, her granola uneaten. It wasn't like she hated him. He just didn't understand why she wasn't happy with him. Everything seemed to be going right. It was his first full time teaching year at Stanford. She was a part time lecturer in the psych department. What was it about *something missing* in her life? She did not come home. He had called the police, but there were no leads at all until someone notified the sheriff that a car had been parked there for several days, near the Mount Tam road. Since then he had been in Mill Valley asking about her, had driven into Stinson Beach and now he was in Bolinas on the off chance that she would have...but he wasn't sure. Why would she have come here? It seemed incredulous, yet her actions seemed incredulous...He would get a room at Smileys, if there was one.

His timing was fortunate. There was one room left, even after an unexpected number of people had come into Bolinas - some asking for rooms - many staying wherever they could put a sleeping bag - the beach being a prime location. The buzz had spread outward and brought in innumerable people ready to crash and wait; wanting to be a part of what was *going down* in Bolinas. This coastal town had become a kind of Mecca and the beach was open to celebration. Even Mariah had gotten caught up in spreading the word. In her case it was through food. She had initiated the soup pot for anyone low on funds and hungry - of which there were many - and let it be known that, "No one was going to go hungry here!" and put a sign on her front window: *Soups on for the Seekers*. The word had definitely spread. And the word was also out that a gathering would occur, on the beach, in the next several days. With that kind of ambiguity the anticipation level grew as to when and who and what. Strange, undecipherable posters had also appeared on telephone poles and unclaimed walls.

Schilling had felt the surge of activity and had tried to calm Damian down by reminding him of their peculiar mission, which was becoming fuzzier day by day. He had tried to bring him back into a Midwestern sensibility by buying him a drink at Smileys.

"Maybe the biker could sober him up," he thought, "or, at least, bring him back to a reality that had some backbone in it."

"Maybe you're going a bit overboard," he finally told Damian, "I do recall that you were easily moved by every cultural period we studied beginning with Woolsey's book on the City of Ur.

That brought a smile to Damian's face as they left their room and headed down the steps to Smileys, maneuvering their way through tunnels of wisteria.

"Woolsey's book was a solid contribution to piquing my interest but it was the odd character who taught the class that brings the subject back. He had a huge head of hair and a walrus mustache that dripped with saliva when he got excited. Remember his description of routine destruction. He would describe years of cultural development, the building of the ziggurats, for example, and 'then the hordes of the East would swoop down and destroy it all', or he would describe the tile work on the Gates of Ishtar and 'then the hordes of the East would swoop down and destroy it all'.

"Except that we have remnants of the ziggurats and the Gates of Ishtar, my dear Damian,

"Yes, but, by God, he loved his subject matter. He would get so excited that by the end of the lecture spittle was drooling down his mustache and dripping onto his notes."

"They don't make them like that anymore, my friend. Even I don't qualify, and you, if you continue on this path, will not reach the level of an eccentric in the Humanities department. You may, however, reach the level of a romantic martyr,

"Don't forget Camus' walk on the beach." Damian countered, "Sometimes we must shoot!"

"Yes, shoot, Damian. You have always had a predilection for immersing yourself in every bygone epoch."

"Why not, every epoch has made its contribution to world culture. And, don't forget, you walked around the Parthenon two times marveling at the *bygone* glory of it until…"

"The hordes of the East would swoop down and destroy it all…"

"Yet, it was not destroyed. For hundreds of years it stood as a monument to the ideals of that by gone classical Greek culture."

"Until Elgin came along."

"Until the cannon ball of the Venetians ignited the powder kegs the Turks stored in it's interior - where Athena once stood."

By now, they had gone past the entrance to Smileys, followed the road along the lagoon, oblivious to all but their abstract reverie of cultural epochs when a voice, like a muted siren, spoke,

"It's an ill wind that blows upon this spot of earth."

They looked to see but saw only an accumulation of cardboard and blankets and seaweed. When it moved they held back. This was not what they had wanted to include in their elucidation of cultural glorification and yet, Schilling couldn't help but respond, "and then the hordes from the swamp came up and destroyed it all."

"It's an ill wind that blows upon the pretense of love."

"Schilling, I think it's trying to tell us something."

"Shall we approach?"

"If we can stand it."

"What are you? Or shall I give you the benefit of our meager doubts, who are you?"

They looked closer to see a woman in the midst of the flotsam tied on her that moved with her.

"Are you by chance the *lady of the lagoon*?" Schilling offered, trying to find some strange humor in this meeting.

"I tell of things to come."

"She's an oracle, Schilling."

"The Oracle of Bolinas."

"And just where do you get your omniscient powers?"

"I am in touch with the incoming and outgoing of the tides. I am Luna the woman of the tides and I feel that which affects the seas of change."

At this point Schilling was ready to move on but Damian felt compelled to ask her, "And what do you see here, Luna? You've said something about an ill wind?"

"I feel the wind of desire growing, yet a dark corrosive current flows under it."

"That's quite a general statement," Schilling responded, "Besides mixing your metaphors, can you be more explicit?"

"All the desire for love will create the illusion of a savior."

"Now, it sounds more like a riddle."

"I feel an inner struggle and a tragic ending."

"And what about a savior?"

"I only feel him and the disillusionment of many."

"Well, that's as clear as this lagoon at low tide. I think I've heard enough."

"Thank you Luna lady, or tidal oracle, whoever you are, don't call us..."

As they turned, the mass of human flotsam slowly blended back into the side of the mesa, the road and the lagoon, her voice still lingering...

"Schilling, don't be too rash with those who see beyond the norm."

"Perhaps, but why does it always seem to come out in riddles or obscure generalities?"

"Such is the history of the seer. Oedipus should have listened to the sphinx."

"At least she was better looking."

"You mean as portrayed by Delacroix?"

"Decidedly, those romantics could embellish anything."

"You're speaking of the French."

"That is true. The German romantics were enamored with Gothic ruins..."

"And the moon, my friend. Do you remember Casper David Friedrich's painting of *Two Men Contemplating the Moon?*"

"Yes, yes, of course. That was one artist I discovered in Nicholson's class. I would say that I found a deeper part of my self in the romanticism of the 19th century, especially the German. Friedrich always painted people looking into the painting, and I felt like I was looking in with them, wondering what they were wondering – the affect of the moon on our actions, the immensity of the universe, or he would paint the left over walls of an old monastery where dedicated monks spent their lives creating manuscripts and embellishing them with knowledge and belief."

"Gone, gone, gone, my friend, except for the manuscripts and the broken down moss covered walls. What is this fascination with ruin?"

"You would say that, and it brings me to our original conversation. You immerse yourself too quickly in the momentary mood or outburst of feeling..."

"Yes, yes, and that will probably be a difference you and I will continue to have, just as I find this oracle of the seaweed having some validity, whereas you have already placed her in some abstract category or psychological pathology."

"You judge me too harshly."

"Ah, but the ability to empathize lies at the bottom of this, and it was probably established in the very early responses of our childhood."

"You mean I responded abstractly and you responded emotionally."

"I mean that early nurturing, the touching, the affection, the physicalemotional development that added to our basic genetic beginning determines how we respond later in life. Empathy comes out of this nurturing and leads to compassion..."

By this time they had come to the door of Smileys' saloon.

"I would like to add to the flow of this conversation. If there is some truth to be found in your ideas, let us peruse it over a dark beer."

"Well, look what the cat drug in." The biker's greeting was barely heard above the din, but Schilling heard it, looked askance at the man and the bar scene regulars and spoke to Damian, "Our friend is, as usual, holding court. Let's pay our respects."

"I presume that was a greeting of endearment?"

The burly biker smiled and responded, "Are you still on the hunt for 'hippies'?"

"We're still doing research."

"Well, you've definitely come at the right time. There seems to be a conflagration of sorts..."

"Mr. Bear, I didn't realize you used the dictionary."

"Jesus, if anybody else had said something like that, I would have stuck a pool cue up his you know what, but you guys frost me...now there's a term you don't hear around here very often and you know why I used it?"

"I'll buy."

"I'll let you in on a little secret. I happen to be from Michigan also."

"What part?"

He leaned closer and whispered, "Frankenmuth."

"No oooo," Damian answered.

"Yea, I've got that Aryan blood in me, so don't..."

"I didn't think anybody left Frankenmuth." Schilling interrupted.

The biker stared at him, "so don't take me lightly."

"We'll remember that. We'd also like a cold one."

"Our turn to buy, actually," Damian remembered.

"You're *act u al ly* on." Bear pronounced with a flare. "Gene, let's have a round for the boys, on our friends, here."

"A round." Schilling added with his eyebrows up.

There was a plethora of appreciation from everybody at the bar. Schilling looked at Damian with chagrin. Damian sighed, but lifted his glass to them, "To the Midwest and the lucky few who left it."

"Here, here..." A clink of glasses and camaraderie ensued. Into this den walked Stanford with his photograph of a dark haired woman wearing a light tan jacket and a gold and brown scarf.

Biker couldn't hold himself back, eyed him and said, "You didn't have to get dressed up for Smileys, mister."

"Sorry, I'm usually a little more casual but," he looked at the biker, looked at us, the rest of the bar, "I wonder if you could help me?"

"What do you need?" Gene, who was listening, responded.

"I'm looking for someone." He held up the photo. "This woman. She's missing. Her car was..."

"She looks good."

"Yes, well, her car was..."

"So what did you do to her?"

"Look, I've haven't heard from her for over two weeks. Her car was found near the Mount Tam highway."

"OK, Ok, let's see the photo." It was passed around and everyone who looked at it either shook their heads indicating no or said something about her looks. Even Schilling and Damian looked at it until Schilling questioned him, "Have you gone to the police?"

"Yes, but no leads at all."

"Has she done this before?"

"No, she..."

Damian interrupted, "You know, a lot of people, seem to be on the road around here...maybe she just wanted to travel..."

"Or maybe, she's joined some religious group...?"

The biker couldn't help but add to the conversation, "Stick around here, mister, maybe she's part of the hippie horde descending on the place. Maybe you could hire these two guys to help you find her."

"I beg your pardon."

"They're doing research on this latest California invasion."

"Actually, we have been taking some notes." Schilling said, as he tried to down play their involvement, but it turned upside down when Damian blurted out, "To tell you the truth I find it all quite exhilarating. I mean I was in the room at the Community Center when this singer turned everybody on, I mean, turned the scene into a kind of smoky revival meeting, it was wild, we were both there and then I was in a room at the Grandiose when this, this same guy, he goes by Shiva, turned the scene into a kind of a sensual encounter, into something out of *1000 and one nights*, it turned out to be onehelluvanight."

The conversation around them quieted down.

"A what?"

Damian knew he was on the spot but couldn't help his enthusiasm...

WOW!

Hold Everything...

WHAT IS IT?
Woke up!
It's 1:22
And I, me, the writer, the author, I have just stepped out of the story to rant in the wee hours…
And I know the…
I know the story was just played out
in the recesses of my mind
in the dreamscape of my mind
Somewhere in my brain is the configuration of the ending of this story in all its tangents
and all its characters
Somewhere…
I know it all just happened
But
I can't get it
I can't access it
I can't access the meaning of it
It's there.
I can feel it
I can taste it.
But I can't get it back…
I can't. The more I try the further it seems to go…
There is …no…more…now…
I'm tired
It's 1:23.
You write it.
You write the goddamn story
Do you read me?
You write it!!!

All right, dear impatient reader, it's been sometime
there's no other way but to try and continue
Or maybe you finished it?
Well, then leave it at that
Read on only to see if…
Only to see what?
That it's all a futile attempt…
At what?
Meaning?
Don't make me laugh?
I'm tempted to tell you that I've thought of some clever way out of this…
the blue haze
Yes
She got a hold of me.
Come on
There you go again
Trying to be clever
When you desperately want to…
I want to say it's something about the past!
Everything you are reading right now is in the past!
No matter how much I want this to be a part of the present, your present…
As soon as you read it, it's in the past – whether it's the beginning of the story in Vermont or the story recollected from Sweet's youth or the halluycischilling or the…
Everything is in the past!
Everything in the past becomes a momentary reality of the present…I call it the persistent presence of the past…and your reading of this, for example, brings it all into the present, into a present reality of meaning…
Now that we understand each other…go on with the story…

"What has be been smoking?" the biker's friend asked.
"Hey, there was something being passed around but it wasn't that, it was

97

more, it was this guy, this singer we heard the other night, it was like he was in a trance and when he came out of it, he had changed, then the room changed, I mean the people in it, he kissed someone on the forehead and they embraced and…"

"Goddamn, he's been brainwashed."

"Hold on, I'm just telling you that the place changed, I felt it, I think everyone there felt it."

"Wait a minute, I get it. This is research, right? Or have you lost it?"

Damian held back from responding. He felt like he had somehow ended up in a tunnel; isolated. He could feel a kind of uncomfortable buildup inside himself. It was a combination of frustration and anger. He did not like being in this position. All eyes were on him. Everyone, it seemed like everyone, out there, was waiting for him to *get with it*. There was something wrong with this. His frustration seemed to come out of what he was feeling, what he had already experienced, something that had touched him in the deeper recesses of who he was as a human being and this crazy interrogation of who he was or more precisely what he felt; what he knew to be true seemed like one of those moments of truth for him and again he was just standing there not responding; afraid to confront…yet, in that moment he remembered another time he had felt a similar conflict. It was when his long ago girlfriend and close friend sat across from him one evening and questioned him about being a prude, about not being sexually enlightened. At that time, he felt something was wrong with their arrogance and yet he didn't respond. He just sat there and let his frustration eat him up.

The irony of this situation, now, was that he felt more enlightened; what had touched him was deeper than what they understood about him…and yet, he was feeling the same kind of frustration again, like being on the other side of arrogant abuse.

At some point in this heavy air, something snapped in him, decorum (even for a bar scene), niceties, manners, fear of not fitting in, all snapped in him, his eyes widened, his muscles tightened, his whole being intensified…

"Not this time!" he yelled out, "None of you know how I feel about this! Do you understand? I could care less about your stupid witless banter, I know what I felt and you, you guys, you can just go to hell, understand, you can just go to hell…"

With that last emphasis, he stormed out of the bar letting the bottom door swing wildly…

This time, even the bar had silenced, and the jukebox seemed on hold, until, finally, the biker said, "Isn't love *loverly*."

Damian had never felt so exhilarated. He was barely on the ground. He had stood up for something that he had felt - no matter what the consequences. He had told them off. He felt free, not just from them and their ideas of him but more importantly, free from his own restrictions, of how he should act. This was a freedom he thought he had, but he realized it was not real until he was put into this excruciating situation. It was then that it mattered to him. This was his crucible. It was as important to him as the greatest of conflicts that any individual might be forced to be a part of and involved in. Maybe the consequences were greater on a worldwide basis but the inner struggle had to be similar and there was the freedom in making a decision. He was acting, not reacting, somehow, now, he felt free to act…and he would find the singer…he would find that girl again…

Schilling finished his beer, said something to the bikers and to the Stanford man and walked out. The Stanford man followed and caught up with him.

"Your friend got a little hot under the collar."

"Yes, he seems to be affected by this *new age* guru of sorts but I think the biker was probably right, he's fallen for some sensuous lips…"

"What's to think of all this?"

"You mean in general?"

"Yes."

Schilling thought for a moment, "One can be on the outside and look at this like any origin of cults throughout our known history. The times create situations that exaggerate or intensify what is lacking in the needs and desires of people, while at the same time, and maybe with a similar energy, it also allows a few people to take up the call and rise up with the answers to those people."

"What about the media in all this?"

"I wouldn't dismiss the impact of the media or technology. The car helped create a youth culture, free from chaperones. The media – from 45's to TV – helped create a common message. In the future the computer and cell phones will make McLuhan's prognostications even more pronounced – the medium will become more and more the message and we will be massaged by each new techno gadget. Remember to add a post World war II explosion of produced things – from housing to dishwashers – all contributing to a material comfort level that had never before happened to so many people…and, of course, we can't forget the atomic bomb which added the discomfort level of annihilation. Combine all that with an adolescent sexual energy and 'voila' you have a witch's brew unlike anything we've seen before."

"That's a pretty good overview. It seems, however, to apply primarily to America and Europe."

"Well, in China, their youth culture is having a Cultural Revolution, promulgated by Mao's socialist and historical philosophy."

"It seems to be turned upside down."

"Yes, while the professors in Berkeley are protesting the status quo of conformity, the teachers in China are being taken out to the farms to get them in touch with their roots - literally – hard physical labor in the rice fields. We can only imagine where that will go?"

"Don't forget there is also a *back to the land* communal movement in this country…"

"Only here, it is by choice."

"Choice is an interesting word. I'm a molecular biologist and human choice is at the basis of my studies. The old conflict of nurture vs. nature is still on a controversial playing field. Obviously, both concepts play a part, it's just how much emphasis we give to one or the other."

"And that has changed over the years."

"Well, we have hundreds of thousands of years of biological evolvement and thousands of years of cultural development and hundreds of years of philosophical attempts at understanding ourselves. These esoteric, mystical, religious, folkloric ways try to explain human nature, the way we act the way we do?"

"And how should we act...?"

"During the last few hundred year's we have gone deeper into our physical make-up, until we succeeded in breaking the code, the blue print of our biological evolvement and probably our thinking."

"A blue print for our thinking?"

"A blue print for our emotions, our intellect, our nurturing..."

"That's definitely a shift in emphasis."

"We've just begun to explain our human actions."

Schilling and Stanford both let that sink a little deeper, as they walked past the young people milling about, some standing in line for free soup at Mariah's, past a group adorned in varied colors singing next to the Shoppe, with a guitarist leading the group in a Donovan song...*yellow is the color of my true love's hair in the morning in the morning when I rise that's the time that's the time I love the best*...now the nasal sound of a kazoo joined in...*freedom is a word I rarely use*...some were just feeling the vibes, enjoying the sunny day...*without thinking oh yea without thinking oh yea of the time of the time when I feel...*

21

Stanford and Julia

Schilling half listened, but his mind was on writing up his notes. He excused himself and went back to his room, his study, his sanctuary, where abstracting was not constantly being interrupted.

Stanford, on the other hand, was also left to his own thoughts, letting the street enter for a while, letting himself be buoyed up by the music, by the words, the laughter, wanting to forget but *wanting to* did not do it, just did not overcome his obsession with Julia, like a scratched 45 he went over and over their relationship. All he could put a finger on was his occasional absentmindedness, but would that really have bothered her – forgetting a luncheon date – or, not remembering what they were going to talk about. Who knows? It was probably kids, though, that seemed to be the ongoing subject and every once in a while she reminded him that they hadn't discussed that possibility since…well, he hadn't said no but apparently he hadn't said the right thing either, maybe that was part of it, she got incensed when he didn't answer her. He could remember, shortly after she moved in, they were lying on the floor, she liked sleeping on a hard mattress so she put his sofa bed mattress on the floor, any way, they were lying there, it was late, the subject of kids had come up, he

101

wasn't ready to discuss it but she just kept prodding him until he clammed up which only increased her frustration or aggression until she literally kicked him off the bed. In this case, off the mattress, which was on the floor, so he didn't have too far to fall. He finally just said *yes* in order to get some sleep. He would have said yes to anything at that point. Looking back on it, he was either a masochist or, or it was a justification, but at that time he felt that he could reasonably talk to anyone or, meet them on some conscious level of respect and basic intelligence. Was this naïve? Some youthful ideal? He didn't think about it in terms of a relationship at that time, He just assumed it was understood, if he didn't have an answer it was all right. He should have realized, from that strange experiences, that their relationship would be different, that he would have to fight for his position on the bed, to declare his position and, if need be, argue it, debate it...She taught him that and, over a period of time, working through their differences, they had found a fairly comfortable day to day living relationship. Beyond that, they were both academically oriented and, he thought, wanted to continue supporting each other in their studies. He thought it was all right; it seemed to be all right. Why did he have to have an answer? But she persisted, and for whatever reasons he hung in there. They had a lot in common and slowly they put their dreams together; he wanted to understand the genetic makeup of emotions, she wanted to study the underlying motivations of human beings and what makes them do what they do...Together they would unravel these human complexities, together...

He had walked up the street without even realizing it. Now, he stood in front of the library, looking into the window, wondering...should he let go? With shelves of books, recollections of hours of his life. What were they now? His eyes closed, he breathed deeply, sighing...the world disappeared...he had finally arrived, he had gotten to a point of no return, when something clicked - a point that clarified the ambiguity, a point where the future was based on an eradication of her memory; the memory of her being meaningful in his life. It was a liberating moment, the weight of all she was in his life was lifted and his future seemed brighter. He sighed again, opened his eyes and was amazed at the life around him. He wanted to walk, he almost bounced off the pavement, began walking around the Mesa along the lagoon until he stopped at the boat launch. He put his arms on the railing, looked out on the depleting lagoon...the light from a snowy white egret bombarded him, almost blinded him. Slowly, his eyes widened and he let the light fill him. It was amazing, he thought, how letting go also opens up an inner space and allows something else to come in, he wanted to say *beauty* but he held back, thinking that somewhere in this was a physicalmental explanation, and he did not want to linger on an academic understanding, he simply wanted to immerse himself in this light, letting the snow white plumage entrance him...letting him forget for a moment...

22

Brown and Gold Scarf

Towards the end of the day, Tamalpais, the princess, was otherworldly, bathed in a soft glow of fading violet, much like the color of the lilacs I picked and gave to my mother on Mother's Day. The pampas grass was lit up like torches in the sun's last rays. Even the beach revelers had slowed down in appreciation – many in reverence of this fleeting moment of beauty, far removed from the agony of armed conflict in Vietnam or the Congo or… The message of the mountain seemed, for many on this beach, to be one of joy, of garlands made from daisies picked in the wild garden a few blocks away and of singing and Frisbees and surfing and the continuous rolling in and out of the surf…Hollywood was beating his drum in the midst of the metal band while at the other end of the beach you could hear conga drums keeping time. Tie-dyed colors of turquoise and magenta and goldenyellow were flying from the 10-foot guitar player while glistening iridescent pieces of abalone shells could be heard tinkling in time – or so it seemed…In the twilight, out of the foment of the never-ending surf, a white bleached piece of driftwood washed up, momentarily holding on to the shifting shoreline. Stuck, rather haphazardly, on one of its sun-bleached branches was a piece of brown and gold cloth. The timing seemed precipitous as Hollywood had ceased his drumming and taken his usual meander along the beach. He was the ancient beachcomber, looking for signs of life from distant shores, something to offer his musicians. Looking into the graygreenwhite movement of the salt water he almost stumbled over the wayward visitor. As he caught himself, his hand fell onto the cloth. He grabbed it... avoiding the white worn branch. Feeling vindicated, he held it up to the remaining light. Within the brown weave were spun threads of gold, a scarf gleaming in the last rays of the sun. They would have to guess his real name before he gave this up. Waving it high, he brought it to the lead guitarist, attached it to a long stick and used that to attach it to the serrated edge of the metal arm. It glistened and waved like a banner of hope as *the evening's empire had not yet returned to sand...*

23

Missing

Stanford slept in fits, turning over, waking up to look at the time – 4:30, 5:30 – waiting for the morning to come, finally 6:30…His window was growing brighter, he couldn't lie there any longer. I'll get some breakfast, he thought, but the street was quiet, no sleeping bags were stirring. He looked into Scowleys and the Shoppe but there were no signs of life. Further down the street, the General Store was closed. Its hour's sign said that it would not open until 8. Next to the door was the community bulletin board that had several layers of local news and posters and notices on it. He scanned their contents for missed connections, missing people, people looking for people:

Peter – lost you at the Donovan concert. Where are you? I want to see you! Debbie

Terry, if you see this, please call home. All is forgiven…your mom.

Notices were of all shapes and materials; from torn brown paper bags to a piece of toilet paper to letterhead paper…this was community communication in a very real sense. He decided to put a notice on the board, maybe a quick drawing of her from her picture. That's what he needed, a few pictures of her up on the local bulletin boards. Suddenly, he was filled with a little more hope; maybe he had gone about this the wrong way. He was not the only one looking for someone, it was possible she just needed to know that he missed her maybe maybe…He went back to his room to write up his appeal to her and to the world:

Missing – Julie - young woman 24. Brown hair, about 5ft 4in with a light tan jacket and a brown and gold scarf. If anyone has seen her please leave message at Smileys. Very important. Stanford

He wasn't sure of the wording but let it go and traced her outline from her picture below the words. When he was somewhat satisfied he brought it to the community board and moved things around until his could be seen and read - until the next concert poster covered it.

Stepping back a few feet, he let her outline blend in with the other notices. He blinked and her outline came back, it was a forest and tree relationship…*What do you focus on?* The lyrics of a song he had written in his high school days, when he was in a rock combo, suddenly came to mind. *What do you focus on?* He had forgotten all about his short attempted foray into the top ten. Even then he realized he was concerned with information, and the catalysts that facilitated the transfer of information, now, looking at the community board, he had one of those light bulb ideas - *that's the direction of the future*. If we could just have them in our hand, somehow he connected to them, I could check Fairfax or San Anselmo or places like Point Reyes Station, odd little spots along the coast, just imagine, I could connect to the Bolinas' personals – people looking for people. He was lost in future thoughts, not noticing the movement in front of the board, several people had passed by, someone in strange clothing, but he was used to that. By the time he focused on the board again he noticed some writing on his notice. Damn, he thought, they wrote over it already, he looked closer and the remains of a magic marker said: *"have seen a brown and gold scarf…"*

He read it out loud, *have seen a brown scarf*…He looked around and yelled out, *"who wrote that!"*

"Check the beach." came a voice from behind the fence.

"What do you mean, *check the beach*?"

No response. He climbed up and looked over the high fence, but saw only an accumulation of flotsam and cardboard. There was no one that he could see.

Where did the voice come from?

Check the beach, he thought, that's the only clue I've gotten so far… *Check the beach*…what the hell does that mean?

24

Procession

A few blocks away, and a few hours later, the creaking of wooden steps, leading from a west-facing room into the kitchen, could be heard. Shiva had put on a white caftan-like robe embroidered with the symbol of the eternal circle around the neck, and was slowly stepping into the role he felt had been destined for him, even with his reluctance and relentless soul searching. The stairs creaked, as they had for others, and he emerged into the waiting eyes of several visitors having tea and engaging in expectant conversation in the kitchen.

"Peace," he said, and raised his right hand with his thumb bent over his little finger and his ring finger, "Peace."

They moved back and gave him room to continue, not out the back door as they had come in but through a kitchen door, which originally opened to the dining room of the old house, and now opened to the renovated store of many trinkets. Val was at the cash register and smiled at the procession. As Shiva walked through, leading the way, he eyed a carved walking stick. It was roughly carved with a globe on the end. He held it. It fit into his palm. He looked at Val, who nodded and, with a grin, said, "It's yours, Shiva, the world is yours."

"Peace to you." Shiva called back as they walked between the newfound old things – another wicker chair, a cabinet, a bookshelf of novels no one had yet wanted, silk plumeria leis were wrapped around a mannequin's neck...He led the way down Main Street with Sweet, Surfer, Damian, Marshall and Jane, who was keeping time with finger cymbals, while a growing number of other interested and bewildered and hepped up human beings followed behind him. Children came out to see the parade and picked flowers along the way to throw in front of him, the Post Office workers came out, as well as the lone real estate agent and someone with a banner with a redorange Zen like brush stroke on it, of an almost closed circle wanting to be closed...It was a gathering storm of laughter, dancing and crazy joy, infecting everyone within ear shot, the word was spreading up and down the streets. Seekers, who were still in the soup line, became aware of something happening, even the bikers, Bear, Gene, the bartender and Sidekick stepped out of Smileys to sniff the air...

Someone turned up the volume of a car radio and the nasal sound of Bob Dylan spread across the street, *something is happening here, and you don't know what it is, do you Mister Jones?*

Something was...and it was not an orderly, military parade remembering old victories, there were no slaves carrying the looted booty of sacked cultures...*hordes of the east*...No, no, no, not here, babe, this, this was a dancing rainbow of joyful people with no borders...When they came close to the greatest expanse on earth, the great Pacific Ocean, it's constant movement lapping on the shore only added to the rhythm of the emerging pilgrims...It's horizon seemed endless as they converged from the street and squeezed through the cement passageway covered with peace signs, yin-yang symbols and words of love to finally emerge into this meeting of landseaandsky, this charged up union of possibility... where some followed some following, passing through, some being born again, opening up to the air, breathing in the air, rich in ions of oxygen that filled the head, the brain, the mind...*if you could read my mind, love, what a tale my thoughts could tell*...Gordon Lightfoot's words wafted on the wind...yes, the mind, the labyrinthine pathways of the mind being studied by Stanford. He caught the word in the air and continued to ruminate on it, as he had on other more studious occasions, the neural connections and synapses – wondering - at what point consciousness, the crux of life? Was it beyond life, beyond nature? Is that possible? If nature has a large enough, wide enough, all-encompassing definition, if it can hold the seeds of a dandelion, the embryo of a human being and the outer regions of the ever expanding universe, then it should include everything...but if nature is limited in its definition, to the biological reality of the earth, then it also limits the explanations and does not adequately answer them...But! How does anyone come to terms with the question: If human beings can imagine and create ideas, are those ideas real somewhere? Are they, in some form or capacity, in this universe, in such a way that they have a reality we can touch on or draw out? In other

108

words, at what point, as our observations of the world become explanations, do our explanations go beyond our observations and become not only beliefs and actualities, and also become the evolution of ideas – the abstract to real development within our brains, mind and consciousness?

Do we always have to come back to 'square one'? Could it simply be the development and evolvement of our brains, primarily our cerebral cortex, a complex cellular structure that, at some point, became a pattern of connections, became a thing in itself (an abstraction)? Maybe, it is just a higher layer of connections? Or is it? Does a certain level of pattern making in the brain become something in and of itself? No, not really, how can it? How can anything be separate from our brain and our mind's understanding of it?

"Enough!" Stanford thought, as his brain and mind finally returned to Smileys. Schilling was leading him out of the swinging doors and into a strangely empty street. "What's going on around here?" he asked Schilling, who also seemed apprehensive.

"I believe it's the harmonic convergence of the stars that has affected this hamlet, this…has become a microcosm of the universe."

"Your sarcasm has a way of letting the air out of their 'happening'."

"Hopefully, it is not just sarcasm but also wit."

"Apparently you differentiate?"

"Well, if wit could feed these starving kids, like it feeds the open mind, then these travelers, these seekers, these hippies would feel a lot fuller than they do…"

"So, what is going to feed them?"

"I fear disillusionment?"

"But isn't much or most of our lives *disillusionment*?"

"Perhaps."

"So what is, and I'm just being a devil's advocate here, what is wrong with youthful reaching, grasping, living for a moment's joy, love, sex, ecstasy?"

"Because none of them last!"

"So, we try to attach ourselves to things, ideas, people that last?"

"Seems that some of us do, eventually."

"Seems, I'm still attached to my wife, can't let her go…"

"You will taste the salt water."

"I beg your pardon."

A voice, coming our of the shadows, repeated the phrase, "You will taste the salt water."

This time Schilling understood the source of the strange gurgling sound and took Stanford by the arm. "The voice belongs to the Oracle of Bolinas," he quietly told him.

"The Oracle of Bolinas?"

"Yes, she's seems to be a part of the flotsam around here, none the less interesting."

So this is what was behind the fence, Stanford thought to himself, telling me to go to the beach.

"We've already had our fortune told," Schilling continued, "or let me put it this way, she has generalized the future around a literate omen, *it is an ill wind that blows.*"

"May I ask what you mean?" Stanford spoke loud enough to reach the mesa hillside.

"Hope and vengeance will beat in the same heart."

"She does seem to speak in generalities. I wonder if you could be more specific?"

"Whatever you seek will bring you anguish."

"Seems like every prognostication you make is tinged in negativity. Is there anything to look forward to?"

"The cosmic record is not concerned with positive and negative. They are all a part of the dance."

Stanford was getting a little perturbed and decided to blurt out his real concern, "Alright, so, will I find my wife or not!"

"You will find hope and vengeance at the same time," she repeated.

"That's the best you can do?"

Whatever movement there was in the shadows stopped and no more sound came from her direction.

"Stanford, I think, we should move on."

"Yes, she apparently lives around here so we could get our fortune told some other time."

Stanford, however, could not, so quickly, let go of the encounter. He did think about his wife and the portents of the oracle, "What did she mean by *hope and vengeance?* Both in the same breath?"

Schilling, too, thought about his friend and his outburst and what it would mean to their friendship, after all, they came here together, but he was primarily concerned with Damian's conversion. "How long would it last?" he wondered.

As they walked past the dentist's office, which was in a house built on stilts sunk into the lagoon, they noticed that the tide had gone out or maybe it was just coming in, right now it was in between and Schilling peered at the soft muddy mushy surface and imagined it changing, being inundated again, the moon's movement would change it again, as it did every day, twice a day, it's unseen force would change the contours of the land and sea. Did this personally affect them? He usually ridiculed the idea. But the tide? This incredibly huge body of water moved every day as a result of the gravitational pull of the moon. "Who came up with this idea?" he wondered, trying to remember an historical observer – Galileo? His mind was reeling now, "Who did she say she was, this lady of the incoming and outgoing tides…come on, this wretched creature, Christ, I'm tired of this…

Be wise, be smart

Be brave my heart

Be…discreet

Stay on your feet

How does Tin Pan Alley come into this? I think sometimes, I've seen too much. I just don't want to put up with this, these idiots; I don't have that kind of empathy…Damian was right about me. I am abstract, I enjoy my music, I enjoy playing a Bach fugue. I like the feel of those pedals and the keyboards and a full open sound with all the stops out, the walls rattling…it's this random, haphazard, anything goes, anytime…

"Schilling!"

The strident call of his name stopped him in his mental and physical tracks. He was inadvertently walking towards the irregularly placed boulders at the end of the road – large breakwater boulders he would have to step around.

"Thank you," Schilling said to Stanford, "My mind seems to have stepped into the 17th century – back to Bach and his Baroque extravaganzas."

"You have a way with words, mister, I don't know your name?"

"It's Schilling, Albert Schilling. And yours?"

"Stephen Stanford."

"Not related, are you?"

"There is a connection, somewhere in the past."

By the time they stepped around the boulders they were inundated with the sounds of drumming. The beat of the congas and the tom-tom had worked its way through the hundreds of revelers. This had become a gathering unlike anything ever seen on the beach of Bolinas. Even Stinson Beach, across the causeway, was silhouetted with people, eyeing the scene. Further south, adding to the larger context, was the ever-present glow of far out near by San Francisco. Stanford and Schilling just took it in, letting dancers twirl around them and pass them by, they could see the metal band in the distance, their abalone shells tinkling in the up draft of the cool sea air, creating an ethereal siren call over the festivities and a lightness to the relenting surf. Fires, set randomly, now illuminated the moving throng, each person illuminated as they moved from darkness into fire light and back again…

112

25

New Age Dionysus

It was...it...how can I describe it, Ellyn reminisced and, for a moment, closed her eyes wanting to let that persistent past formulate and rise into the present, it was such a time...you have to imagine...even then your imagination can only take you so far – if Marcel Ophuls, Kurasawa, deMille, David Lean, Murnau, Herzog made a film of this time, this day, maybe then you could get an understanding or a feeling of the spectacle played out on the beach of Bolinas at that time. Imagine the waves lapping on this shore of revelry – Dionysus in the new world, not on the edge of the Acropolis but reborn on the sand below the mesa of precarious sandstone. It was as if this God had been reincarnated in the form of a lean, bearded, longhaired young man, now holding court in the midst of a circle of torches, their fire flickering, encircling him and his followers. He sat on Indian batik sheets leaning against white pillows. Jane Caravan, who was now calling herself Sunburst, sat near by, occasionally shaking her prayer rattle or making high pitched sounds with the brass bowls surrounding her, each bowl had a different pitch, a siren sound...enticing, cajoling, eerily pulling everyone within ear shot towards this metaphoric island – surrounded by soft sand on which to languish or cutting coral on which to be ripped apart. Surfer had become Shiva's right hand helper. Sweet was bringing followers or curious onlookers into the circle one at a time to greet the new messiah. He opened his arms to all who came to him, held their face in his hands and kissed them on the forehead intensely whispering *live in ecstasy* as he looked them in their eyes. Many of the curious who had come into his circle looked at him and felt touched by this momentary experience; enough to want more. It was as if he charged them with something…some were receptive to him and his evocation, others left half wondering at what this scene was all about.

Marshall was still living in the after thoughts of his encounter with him. He could not get the experience out of his mind. It had started to consume him to the point that he wanted to be reminded of that moment - the total immersion into a deep ecstatic living force that he had experienced. His role, too, was to bring potential followers into the fold. He seemed almost obsessed with the repeated oration of his baptism. At one point he took a red hot stick out of the fire he was tending, held it up and announced that this was the validation of his experience, the moment to be seared into his palm, to remind all who knew him and who would know him that he had touched ecstasy; that he had been touched by one who could bring ecstasy into his life…In the frenzy of that moment he stuck the heated stick into his palm and cried into the sky – *aieeeeee*…a cry, not of a flesh pain, but of primordial pain, in which all his life forces became concentrated…his cry resounded around him and only heightened the desires of those coming from Shiva's sanctuary. One wide-eyed seeker came to Marshall and held up his palm. Marshall pulled the reheated stick from the fire and thrust it into his palm. His cry pierced the night…upon which the intermittent cries of other followers were added to the crescendo of pain and joy dancing in the firelight… primordial pain and momentary, almost desperate, joy pierced the smoky air and overlapping waves…

At the other end of the beach, where the metal band was playing a long extemporaneous riff, Schilling was still keeping his distance, even as rainbow colors swept past him, catching Frisbees or flying a kite or dancing to the conga beat pulsing over the sand. Hollywood had momentarily left his drumming and was engrossed with several of the initiated followers. They were holding up their palms in a consecrated dignity, as if tuned to a gesture or a scar from an earlier time – a dueling scar or the scarred remains of an Indian war dance. He looked warily at their burnt offering. He even understood their desire, but could not help remembering his grandfather's words, "Ritual goes deeper than skin, it is our connection to past generations."

Their desire seemed real, he thought, their circular wound was part of their realm and their enthusiasm seemed to be real yet…something was grating on him. Was it his usual underlying lingering loss – the justification for his usual drunken state or was there something about this gathering that he understood that brought about this unease?

"What were these kids doing?" He wondered. At the same time he also didn't mind the attention...He was a star, after all, and they were recognizing his status...They were coming to him to sanctify their conversion.

Stanford, too, found him interesting, but in his eyes, this tom-tom pounding left over from a bygone history was not a vessel of traditional wisdom or a symbol of bravery but a curiosity to put up with, for what ever information he might have, since he lived on the beach. Stanford closed in on the small crowd, interrupted them with his, by now, mantra of request: "Excuse me but I wonder if I could ask you something?" Hollywood turned to him. The others did also, thinking he wanted to know about this earth shaking event they were a part of..."I'm looking for a woman, going on 24, here is her picture...

He wanted to show them but they just looked at him. He held the photo up and passed it in front of their faces. They smiled. Hollywood finally said, "She could have been anyone of the hundreds here today, Mister. You might just have to open your eyes."

"Maybe, you should see the Messiah?" someone said, Maybe he could help you find her."

"Messiah," he repeated, "what now?"

"He is incredible..."

"Take the photograph..."

"Go to him, he won't refuse..."

Stanford looked around for Schilling. He saw him sitting there, on a wave-beaten log, in the midst of several dogs, seemingly oblivious, his pipe lit...surveying the scene like a traffic-watch helicopter, seeing but not a part of the dancing or the drama.

"Schilling!" Stanford yelled, "Let's go see the wizard." As soon as wizard was heard several branded followers offered to lead them.

"We can take you to the wizard but we prefer to think of him as the messiah..."

"Who is this messiah?"

"He can touch you and everything becomes one, a heightened one, another state of one, an ecstatic one..."

Stanford shook his head, "What are you going on about?"

"We've touched him, he's touched us...somehow something happened, man, I can't explain it, but my whole body started to feel like jello, like a wave was going through me, I was moving and it felt like I was being born, like life was coming into me, man, talk about ecstatic...

"Talk about, wow, hey, what have you got to loooooooooose?" The loooooooose resounding into the sky and back to the sand...back to the followers now leading them, like a conga line, they snaked their way through the blankets and fires and kids and dogs, past the break water, to the circle of torches, now surrounded by enough branded followers to make them wonder about this phenomenon, this new-age messiah that they had heard enough about.

"Schilling," someone called out, while they were standing in line. It was

Damian, dressed in billowing white cotton pants with a fuchsia colored nightshirt, a long red scarf flowing from his neck. Schilling and Stanford just looked at him, holding back any immediate response.

"It looks like you've come to the source – not a bad idea for the research."

"Damian, don't tell me you've gotten branded too?"

Damian held up his palm and showed them the circular burn not yet healed.

"It looks like you've made an existential leap."

"Yes, this time I did it. And you?"

"Research, my dear, lost friend, research...we've been talked into seeing this seer of yours."

Stanford added, "We, that is, I am going to ask him about my wife."

Marshall came to them, looked questioningly at them and asked,

"You have come to see the messiah?"

"Yes, actually, we'd like to ask him something."

Marshall felt uneasy but directed them slowly into the midst of the circle. They could see Shiva close to Sweet laughing lightly, an intimate exchange that had an affect on their mood, their impulse to get in, ask questions and go on. Maybe it was the torches, the questioning, the darkness, or the cooling air or a feeling of reverence, but both Schilling and Stanford were more contemplative when Shiva finally looked at them and smiled, "Sit down, gentlemen. I've been waiting for you." They looked at each other and tried to make themselves comfortable on several of the pillows strewn about.

"Why have you come?"

Stanford was the first to respond, "I, I was hoping you could help me find someone?"

"I think I'm better at helping someone find themselves."

"And how do you that?" Schilling asked somewhat sarcastically, "In fact, I'm just curious, how did you take this on?"

"Take what on?"

"This role, this gurumessiah role?"

"Did you come to ask me that?"

"No," Stanford said.

"Yes," Schilling said, more to his friend than Shiva.

"I just want to find someone." Stanford responded.

"And, I guess I want to know how you found yourself or, to put it into the generic, how one finds oneself?"

"I think we have two streams running side by side," Shiva answered. As he said this he remembered his own mind traveling on two separate paths, becoming one...

"Maybe they converge at some point."

Schilling was not ready to let his inquiry be sidetracked. He looked Shiva in the eyes and asked, "What prompted you to take on this role?"

Shiva was slow to answer, his face almost contorted in thought, "I can only answer the needs of those who listen to me."

"At least you're honest about it, but don't you feel some kind of responsibility to those, to these kids who are looking of something, for someone…?"

"I am one of the answers."

"Damn it man, there are kids out there who are branding themselves…for some reason that has to do with you."

"I did not ask for that."

"You apparently tell them to become irrational, telling them that they'll achieve ecstasy of some kind…"

"And you want less than that?"

"Be reasonable, no one can live in ecstasy all the time. At some point it, or the state of ecstasy fails…"

"So, failure is to be avoided?"

"Yes, no…"

"No, recognition of the consequences shouldn't be avoided."

"Is ecstasy, even for a moment, to be avoided?"

"No, yes…"

"Who's gonna pick up these kids when it wears off?"

"Life will continue! And some will have lived with a greater intensity and awareness than others."

"So, that's it, if someone dies tomorrow, or tonight it will all be the same to you. As long as they've lived with that moment of awareness or ecstasy as you've put it…"

"Every moment of concentrated life is to be valued. It can be like that moment when the possibility of death stares you in the face."

Stanford finally interrupted the exchange, "You're not going to get anywhere with this. Please, may I ask you something?"

Shiva and Schilling looked at him as if he had just broken a spell – a verbal ritual that had a reference to the beginning of consciousness. It was a dialogue of awareness; what it means to experience life.

"Look, please, can you look at this photo and tell me if you've seen this woman?"

Shiva smiled with indulgence at his insistence, "All right, let me see it…"

Stanford held the photo in front of him. They both watched his reaction. At first, they were taken back when he seemed to freeze, his jaw tensed…

"Well?"

Finally, through half-closed eyes, he said,

"She looks like any other young woman who has come here, if she changed her clothes and let her hair down."

"So, you haven't seen her. She disappeared some weeks ago. I'm her husband. You've seen quite a few people these last few days…Maybe…"

"She looks like someone out there." Pointing to the myriad dancers and revelers he finally said, "I don't know her."

"OK, OK, I don't know if you've seen her or not. Don't you give direct answers?"

Schilling responded this time, "I don't think you're going to find her here."

117

Stanford glared at him.

"It is apparent she isn't gone," Shiva finally said, "You can't seem to let her go..."

"Don't tell me what I can't let go." He snapped back.

"Be cool," Marshall added when he heard the tone of the exchange, "Put your energy into finding her, not finding someone to blame or get angry at."

"That's the smartest thing I've heard all night," Schilling quipped, trying to get Stanford to calm down, "Let's go..."

He turned to Shiva, "I hope you know what you're doing."

"We all do what we are capable of...you, too, are capable of more." were his parting words to Stanford and Schilling.

As they left the circle of fire light, Damian caught up with them, "Well, what do you think, is he the real thing?"

Schilling's immediate response was "He's either a charlatan or an opportunist. Either way, he's..."

Damian cut him off, "Sometimes being cynical doesn't cut it anymore Schilling, he's touched a lot of people. Look around you. They're feeling things they've never imagined..."

"Yea, like a hole in their palm. You've lost it, Damian."

"Schilling, damn it, man, you're wrong. I finally found it." As he said this he turned to young girl next to him and smiled.

They both nodded in recognition of what that look meant. As he turned Stanford took the connection one step further and said to all of them, "I'm heading back to Smileys. I do believe I've had enough for one night"

The beach had gotten darker, fires were burning out, embers were glowing and reflected in the eyes of many who were still sitting and lying around, guitar strumming could be heard and the occasional lyric resounded over the sand, this one by a singer whose time had come, *I'm the Pied Piper, follow me, yes, I'm the Pied Piper, don't you see, I'm the Pied Piper, and I'll show you where it's at...*

26

Confrontation

"Let's take one last walk through the crowd," Schilling said to Stanford, "You never know."

By the time they meandered their way back to the metal band, the tom-tom had stopped...

"Maybe, you should see the Messiah!" someone shouted again,

"Maybe he could help you find her."

"Messiah," he repeated and yelled back, "I've seen the messiah and he's not my savior!" He looked around at the upraised palms and heard the band rattle. The banners were still flying. One banner caught his eye. It had a shimmer of gold reflecting off the open flames of Hollywood's dying fire. Somehow he could not break his gaze – his eyes were cemented to this flopping flying banner.

"Where did you get that gold and brown scarf?" he finally blurted out. His voice seemed outside of him – like the voice of a dummy in the hands of a ventriloquist. They stared at him and then looked at the scarf flying in the evening sea breeze.

"Where did you get it?" he yelled at Hollywood.

"It was on the beach, that's where all that stuff came from."

"It's hers. I would know it anywhere. Schilling!" he looked around, "Schilling!" he yelled again.

Schilling came to him.

"Look, it's her scarf flying from that contraption, that metal grating." He couldn't hold back and started towards the band overwhelming him. Hollywood moved between him and the metal guitarist, now clicking with abalone shells. It was dressed in dried seaweed and rocking with a gold and brown flag of distinction.

"You're not going anywhere." Hollywood glared at him.

"I want to see that scarf!" he voiced with such determination that Hollywood lifted his hand to hold him back.

"That stays on the guitarist."

But Stanford's mouth pursed. He felt the anger rising in him. He was not in a patient mood.

"Get out of my way, you crazy drunk."

The crowd forming around him were calling out *peace, be cool*...but he pushed Hollywood out of his way and grabbed the metal legs of the guitarist shaking the rickety connections until the abalone shells fell off like large hard pieces of confetti. He pushed off a leg until the figure was beginning to tilt...

Hollywood staggered over to Stanford and grabbed his shirt collar from behind. Stanford, infuriated now, turned and smashed his fist into Hollywood's red nose. He reeled back with redder blood gushing out.

Several people grabbed Stanford's arms and someone held him around the neck. He struggled and threw them off. He did not realize his own strength as he tackled the tilting ten-foot high metal figure. His whole body went into the once famous beach musician and slowly it went back wards, falling, all eyes on its slow demise until a crash of metal and wood resounded over the revelry – everyone looked in the direction of the band and wondered if this was the finale to a great concert...

Stanford did not wait for an encore or the sand to settle. He ran to what was the arm and untied the gold and brown scarf.

"This is hers!" he yelled. "This is hers," he said again, only quietly, with a questioning voice. He closed his eyes, holding the scarf, feeling the texture, the gold straws woven into its weave.

The abalone shells were strewn in the sand. The waves had stopped, no one moved...Even Hollywood held back...It was like the conclusion of a great work of music with everyone in such a state of shared experience that they did not want to break the silence outside of them, their inner experience being so full of sound. In that sense, except for Schilling, no one understood the facets of his statements, but the emotion of the question had become theirs, theirs, until a roving dog came to him, while he was kneeling on the ground, holding the talisman of fabric. Everything came back, everything started again, the dog sniffed the fabric...

"Here, here," he held it under the nose of the dog, "here, smell it, take me to her..."

The dog yelped and ran to Hollywood.

Stanford looked up, he was not looking for facts or making researched conclusions, his intellectual conclusions were couched in other parts of his brain. He thought of himself as a scientist, a molecular biologist, a student of the workings of the brain but he was still a combination of all the evolved conditioning of 100,000 generations of Homo sapiens...

He looked at Hollywood, his eyes bulging, "What have you done to her?" With that question something changed in the crowd. It was an accusation thrown out like a spear or more like a shot from a Colt 45.

Hollywood, (had he not weathered enough shots, fallen from enough horses?) was still reeling from the real fist. He saw Stanford get up, holding the scarf, and walking towards him, "Did you take this off of her? What did you do with her?"

The buzz began around him, "What is he talking about? Who is this guy?" Hollywood wasn't sure what to make of him. He was holding his nose, still trying to stop the bleeding. He finally got some words out, "I found this scarf on the beach."

"Like hell you did. You found it on her. What did you do with her?" He rushed at him again. Several people ran in front of Hollywood. Schilling tried to stop Stanford, "Calm down, Stanford, Jesus. Lets do this differently...Let's get the cops on this." He held him by the arm and dragged him towards the road.

"We've got to strike now!" Stanford said making a halfhearted attempt to go back.

"Tomorrow, we'll get the sheriff or the local police, at least you have something to go on..."

27

Pilgrim and Demigod

Evening's revelry and revelation finally gave way to the calming consistency of the rolling waves, not seen anymore but heard, a reminder of the larger rhythms. The circle of initiation had grown dark, the torches had burned out, only the embers of a few bygone fires still glowed sporadically on the sand. Shiva and Marshall, Sweet and Surfer, Damian, Tanya and Jane were heading back to the Grandiose. Others of the entourage had spread their sleeping bags out and settled in or essentially, settled out for the rest of the night. For the first time, questioning thoughts had strayed into Shiva's mind. As he walked back to the hotel he was more than unusually quiet. His companion's considered him contemplative, but his thoughts were on the photo shown to him by Stanford. "Was this woman someone he had met, touched, kissed? Was this the same woman? He had seen people change in front of him, in his embrace, in their eyes, he thought he was living in the *now* and bringing others into what he had seen and what he hoped was an ecstatic state of being. What did this photo have to do with him? What did his past have to do with him? Now that he had realized the present, what did he have to do with a past that most people cling to, a past that

123

they live with and most of the time would not want to deny, obliterate, change or forget...what did he have to do with those people or those events, or that photo or that woman?"

In his revelry, he remembered a Zen koan, one that always made him think, one that seemed to break his routine response to a situation...He saw a master walking down a path with a devotee. They came across an old man at a stream. The devotee passed him and the master picked him up and carried him across the stream. Later, down the path, the devotee asked him why he had broken his meditative walk to pick up the old man? He answered, "I dropped off the old man on the other side of the stream, you are still carrying him...

How long would he carry that woman? Was he not beyond that? Could he not just drop her off? Each question brought a slight quiver to his being, a pin prick to his certainty, yet to his friends he was in a contemplative mood, quiet, purposeful...his steps measured...

"What a day," Sweet broke the silence.

"And night." Damian added.

"And what a time for us to create again..." Shiva stated, his voice overly strong, as if to convince himself as well as the others that his insight was real, that it touched on higher knowledge. Inside, however, he felt a slight wavering, a questioning...his mind wondering...*to feel the upwelling of inner life is in itself ecstatic* he thought, and let himself carry a lighter load...*to experience a sun drenched moment in the garden of a local café when the afternoon light breaks through the trellis to warm your face – this, this is our connection to ecstasy, this moment of cosmic connection – the sun, our sun, our star and life-giver...the ancients recognized it, they recognized that an ecstatic state could bridge the gap to this primal power; that the ritualistic use of mind-altering drugs and sexuality could possibly let them touch that primal state...would these young people let him add rituals to their experimenting? Would they take the time for initiation? Or was that a time that was? He tried to make sense of his inner wanderings and for the first time questioned his role in their lives...their lives...their lives...their lives...he repeated with each step...*until the night air and the evening sky with diamonds dazzled him...and the closeness of their bodies jostled him into being there, walking strolling towards their Grandiose refuge...

After they had ascended the stairs with all their attendant creaks and settled sounds, Shiva's thoughts again turned to his followers. Inside the room their faces were now contrasted between the single source of light and their myriad shadows. He could see Marshall's face unusually highlighted, reflecting his strength and his softness, his vulnerability.

"Marshal, look at me." Shiva instructed. "Your fire comes from a deep place inside you, yet, I wonder what feeds it? Or how long it will last?"

Marshal was taken aback for a minute. He was usually the questioner of others and had been the instigator of any number of personal encounters since the night Shiva held him and kissed him on the forehead. Yes, he was driven by something inside him, his - and this was always close to

124

the surface - his upbringing. His mother had put her life into him. His father had left him at an early age. Everything he was, it was because of her, at least, this is how he felt; this is what she had told him in any number of ways. As he got older, she let him know how important he was in her life, he was the man she had lost and did not want to lose again. He loved her but could not reconcile his own needs to grow, to establish himself...he used the money she had worked for, had sacrificed for, to go to Columbia and eventually get a degree in sociology. He could, at least, be a social worker. It seemed like his home life had prepared him for interpersonal conflict through his search to try and understand their relationship. At one point he mentioned to his mother that he was considering moving into a flat with roommates. He would have his own room, but that didn't make sense to his mother, "Why would you want to move into another room when you have one here? Would they cook for you? Who would cook latkes for you? Who would clean up after you? Over dinner they discussed or argued this possibility and by the time he went to bed it was all settled. There was no reason to move.

As a result, the years went by, his record collection of classical music grew, especially his Baroque brass collection, his forays into one social group after another fed his needs to confront others and every confrontation seemed tainted with his mother and their relationship. After one, particularly intense session of 'rebirthing' he was determined to make a change in his life – he had been reborn – at his age.

At home, after his mother had gone to bed, he packed some clothes, a few books and a few well-chosen records and wrote a long note, to his mother. He decided to leave before she woke up, before he could second-guess himself and turn back. Before he knew it, he was looking in the mirror, in the cramped bathroom of an Amtrak train, click-clacking its way to San Francisco.

He took on the local culture, just like he had taken on his personal confrontations in New York. He was drawn to dance, that had been his secret dream, to be a member of Martha Graham's dance troupe or Merce Cunningham's or even Diaghilev's. To dance to Stravinsky's music, to become the fawn in the afternoon, this had been his dream even if his body had grown sluggish, in his mind he could dance. In his footloose explorations of San Francisco he was a dancer. On one occasion he was with two friends, after a Stuttgart Eurythmy performance at the Opera House, they stopped in at a local ice cream parlor on Market Street. Coming from inspired movement and hearing Sinatra's *Strangers in the Night* on the jukebox he took Brenda's hand and they proceeded to do an impromptu dance in the middle of the parlor. It was one of those moments that transformed the immediate scene. They danced until the voice died and they lay prone on the floor...the few patrons watching, gave them a rousing applause.

That was all before Bolinas, and yet, it was with this sense of immediacy that Marshall was drawn to Shiva, who seemed like a kindred spirit in his advocacy of 'being in the moment' and his desire for the ecstatic state of being. Marshall wanted, not only ecstasy, but also relief from his ever-constant underlying desperation to be at peace with himself, without guilt. Now he was in the company of someone who had helped him forget, who had brought him into the present, even more, who had touched his inner desires. He would bring others into this circle...and during their slow walk back to the Grandiose, he realized the circle had already grown larger. Even when the core group that accompanied Shiva had, momentarily, retreated into their own separate worlds he felt there was something, maybe in their steps, maybe in their awareness of each other, that seemed to encompass them, to connect them...

Sweet, too, had felt a connection during their short jaunt homeward and as this feeling of being together swept through her, her eyes had widened. She looked at Surfer. He caught her glance and they both smiled – a feel good smile. She had reached her arm into his, held him as they walked, speaking softly to him saying, "Let's go somewhere tomorrow, just the two of us..."

He smiled and nodded, "I know where there's a waterfall, up the coast, falls right onto the beach. It's a bit of a hike..."

"Sounds great! I could use a good long walk, especially if we end up on some wild spot."

Before their gaze had broken off they were at the Grandiose joining the circle, embracing the others enveloping Marshall while Shiva welcomed everyone to spend the night.

28

True Love

It was early, before the room stirred with visitors hoping to meet the new messiah. Sweet nudged Surfer and reminded him of their plans to hike to the waterfall. She tickled him to get him to move. Knowing he didn't want to wake up Shiva, his face contorted trying to stifle his laughter. He moved faster and before she could turn around he grabbed her hand and was pulling her towards the door, both taking quick steps down the creaking staircase. The air in the kitchen had cooled from the open door to the back yard. "They leave the door open all night," she thought, what a place, it's just open to the world, if someone wants some water or tea, they can just come in...

They warmed their hands around cups of Morning Zinger and let the stillness linger. Surfer caught her eyes and Sweet turned into a smile, a sweet innocent smile that touched him, until they both felt the warmth of being close and something welling up inside of them – *young love, first love* – wafted through the air – *filled with true emotion* – the kind of love that was on the air waves somewhere in the world and sung by crooners

and teenage idols and one hit wonders and the occasional archetype who seemed to mouth the inner desires of a generation. Somehow all the songs of teen-age love resonated in her smile, in their eyes, in his face…
"Let's go," she suddenly said to him. They practically ran out of the kitchen, down the drive way and along the street, turning left onto Mesa Road, still running with a kind of unbound excitement until Surfer slowed down, looked at Sweet and said, You know, it's quite a ways to the beach."
"You mean, maybe we should slow down and walk…or hitch hike?"
"I mean, yea, love, it's a long ways before we even get to the beginning of the trail. It's great though; you go by two fresh water lakes, right by the ocean. We can go for a swim and the lakes are near the cliffs and…" He was getting all worked up, his pace quickening, when a pickup slowed down enough for Sweet to put out her thumb. The driver stopped and they climbed in the back.
"We're heading for the waterfall on the beach." Surfer yelled out to be heard over the motor.
"Well, I'm going as far as the bird sanctuary. There's a bit of a walk to the trailhead."
"That's all right, we have all day."
They settled into the cargo space, leaned against the cab, letting the potholes and the driver's attempt to avoid them, become a jostle that occasionally brought them closer. They smiled, laughed, let their bodies touch, an erratic jostle became erotic in the back of this pickup, open to the blue sky and receding eucalyptus trees. In a calm moment Surfer looked at her, touched her cheek and when the truck bounced his finger poked her eye.
"Auau," she winced.
"Oh, god, I'm sorry."
"It's all right, Surfer," she said and laughed. She took his hand and pressed it against her cheek. He closed his eyes, just to feel her soft skin, her face. She turned and kissed him. The pickup lurched but their lips only grew closer. Through bumps and careening movement they were glued to each other. Each bump made them hold on tighter. *Stuck on you* Surfer thought of Elvis, *wild horses couldn't pull us apart…"*
"Here's where I turn off," the driver yelled out the window. They did not hear him. They did not want to separate; they were in a separate world.
"Hello, young lovers," he said in a softer tone. Here we are…where are you?"
They were in a small parking lot next to a sign that said – California State Bird Sanctuary. Before they saw the first bird, they had hopped out of the truck and thanked the driver. Just as they were to continue on, he asked them if they would like to go on a round of bird sighting with him. They looked at each other, shrugged their shoulders, decided yes and, out of curiosity, enthusiastically joined him.
The path led into taller trees, spanned by netting that their guide looked at and seemed to listen to until some commotion could be noticed in a

128

small section. He went to it and cupped his hands around fluttering wings. Captured by unnoticed filaments of string a wild free flying bird had flown into what, obviously, was not in its recognition of danger. He cuddled the tiny fluttering feathered being until only a head with a small down-turned pecking beak shown through. Its eyes alert. What was it thinking? Their guide gently stroked its head, trying to calm its hypersensitivity...gently, one stroke after another, until calmness pervaded around it and all of us.

"It's a finch, fairly common," He allowed one wing to protrude through his fingers in order to measure it and count the feathers. "We're trying to track the local population and the migrating birds. This band that I'm putting on will allow us to track it."

"Until the next time it flies into a net." Sweet added.

"Yes."

"Maybe it will learn from this and not fly into another net."

"Would you like to hold it?"

Sweet's eyes opened up in anticipation. "I'd love to."

"Cup your palm and gently but firmly close you hand around her body, especially her wings. You have to make her feel secure."

"You know it's a female?"

He shook his head and slowly handed the bird to Sweet. Hesitating at first, she slowly put her hand around her feathers, letting her head poke out...until exaltation and anxiousness swept over her.

"I can feel it's heart beating...It's like having life itself in my hand...jeez, a life I could crush so easily and yet it's softness, it's fragility, it's..." She stood there, with Surfer's arm over her shoulders. "It's like being trusted with something. It's pulse, it's slight heaving of life."

"And you determine its freedom to fly," Surfer added.

"That's a very important point," the ranger said, "We are a part of their world and how we respond to their life, their cycles and their food chain, can determine how they will live in that freedom. Its not just holding them securely but letting them fly in the security of a larger hand – the air, the land, the water. We are a part of the larger hand holding this fragile being – with all the input of six billion people, twelve billion hands in need and plenty all holding a fragile living feathered being.

Surfer acknowledged the ranger's worldview, yet also felt strange, almost embarrassed by Sweet's sentiments. He couldn't let go of her. No girl, he knew, had expressed this kind of sensitivity, in such an open, feeling way. He was drawn to her; he wanted to hold her, hold her like she held the bird. All these forever feelings, however, landed back on earth when their guide had finished writing the data of this quivering specimen.

"We are done with this one. You can release her."

As soon as he heard 'release' Surfer's thoughts went to the words of a Dylan song,

I see my life come shining
From the west coast to the east
Any day now

Any day now
I shall be released
Sweet and Surfer held their breath while her hand slowly opened. She felt the air on her wings and swiftly took to the sky.

"Goodbye, beating heart," Surfer said to the diminishing flutter of wings. They followed the speck for a long time until Sweet turned to the Ranger, "Can we come again?"

"Hey, you're always welcome, we could use some volunteers. You know, we have plans to build a visitor center, and..."

Surfer cut him off, "Sounds great, but I want to show her the water fall, if we can make it..."

"You know, you helped out. I'll take you to the trail head, otherwise, it'll be dark before you come back."

"Jeez, thanks, what's your name, by the way?"

"Jagermeister, Wilhelm, but most people call me Wild."

"Wild?"

"Yea, I was, at one time, I did my share of destroying things, until I had an epiphany."

"What do you mean?"

"Well, we used to go out and shoot things, with bows, we made our own arrows, anyway, we had to practice so we shot anything that moved."

"Why?"

"Who knows, we were caught up in it, practicing for deer hunting, well one day we were out target practicing in this canyon when I saw something move under a bush. It looked like a rabbit. I pulled back my bow and aimed my two inch tri-blade arrowhead and let go..."

"And?"

"I got it, went over to pick it up. I was a baby rabbit still quivering. The arrow had pinned it to the ground. I felt sick. I didn't want to touch it. I never felt so bad in my life."

"God, how terrible."

"After that, I never wanted to kill anything again. I still went deer hunting but never took a shot. I just walked when I could. To see deer grazing in an open dappled clearing become almost sacred for me. Sitting in the stillness let me hear the forest for the first time; it was amazing, the birds and animals that would occasionally come into that space. I listened and wondered...I think it was there that I decided to become a protector of wildlife."

"What a story."

"Yea, well, I'm still called 'Wild' but it refers more to wild protection. By the time he had finished they were at the trailhead. They said thanks and he told them to stop by the sanctuary again. They walked the narrow trail, at times lost within the high grasses. It was, as Surfer remembered from his childhood with his father, a mysterious pathway. On one of their hikes, he had lagged behind his father and somehow took the wrong turn or walked through some opening in the grass, maybe a deer trail...in any case he remembered going deeper into the grass until he was engulfed

130

in a tunnel that seemed without end, yet finally ended in a small opening encased by several low growing pine branches. The ground was soft with pine needles. He was tired and lay down on the bed, still warm from some living thing – at that time he sensed the comfort of the earth and the warmth of coursing blood. Now, he could talk of *blood consciousness* and the immersion of life with life in all its sensual and sometimes cruel beauty. Then, he was, or at least he remembered, letting the aroma ooze into his very pores, the consciousness of pungent pine and musty dry grass, while the give of the earth, layered with years of dropped and dried needles, became a soft bed for him. He wondered how something so sharp could also create something so comforting, so all enclosing. He curled up and fell into a sleep, deeper than he could remember, where dreams create a reality so intense that every smell, every slight movement of air could be felt and yet, he could also be suspended in some transitory space, floating in a nether world with all senses intact. Here was his past, no; here was a timeless world, in the womb of space…a dream world somehow there in his mind, a world of his own making, lost…"where are you? Come back baby…" Sweet's voice added to his floating world and crept in, becoming a part of him until his eyes slowly gently opened to his place of refuge.

"Sweet," he murmured, "hold me." He wanted her. He could almost feel her. "Sweet," he cried out, "Where are you?"

She heard but could not see. His voice came through the tall grass. He was there, but where?

"Sweet!"

She heard and separated the stalks of grass and bushwhacked or weedwhacked her way through…

"Sweet."

Changing direction she cocked her ears to hear his voice again. "Surfer," she responded, "Where are you? I'm coming."

Before her name resounded again she saw him and went to him, surrounded him with her arms, he let her in until they rolled and rocked in the pungent pine with all the variations of a concerto for two instruments from the first movement of desire to the slow movement, the adagio of touching to the final crescendo of their movements; that ecstatic place that stops time, after which the coda let them simply lie together, be together, as so many had before them…as Leonard Cohen so beautifully stated in those wondrous days of yore, *and you want to travel with her and you want to travel blind and you think maybe you'll trust her because you've touched her perfect body with your mind…*

131

29

Roderick

The news had penetrated Smileys. With much swagger and delight Bear and his friends had listened to Stanford's encounter with Hollywood which just added froth to the beer being consumed...He had told it numerous times and, in fact, was now soused enough to either forget everything that ever happened to him or roused up enough to wake the entire community, "The hell with it all..." he yelled and shook his head. "I'm gonna fucking squash that bastard...if he's done anything to Julia! I'm gonna..." His voice rang out but his legs weren't following. Before he could say anymore he had fallen into the hands of Bear and Schilling. They held him up and walked him to his room. "I'm gonna getta getta..." he slurred, until his face hit the pillow and sleep closed his wound... Morning came with a loud banging on his door and the strident voice of the deputy sheriff, the same deputy who had roused Shiva and Sweet from their sleep when they first set foot in Bolinas "Stanford, is there a Stanford in there?"

"Wha," was all he could muster.

"Open up, its Roderick, the deputy sheriff..."

"Uh, ach, OK, I'm coming…"

He rolled out of bed, hit the floor, got up, staggered to the door and opened it.

"You were going to meet me at Mariah's, remember. I didn't think I'd have to track you down."

Yes, he was to meet Stanford at Mariah's in the morning. Bolinas was his territory and over the years he had had a love and hate relationship with the old Bolinas, the old guard, the original iconoclasts of the town. Now it had expanded to include all the lost kids congregating in and around west Marin. On the one hand his threat to make it difficult for any wayfarer coming through his territory usually got him a payoff in grass which made it easier for him to do his job, that is, drive the back roads or watch the sky or have coffee at any number of cafes. On the other hand he sometimes compensated for his guilty feelings about not carrying out the law, as he had, at one time, sworn to do, by realizing that this was Marin in the new age. Here, even the law allowed for some flexibility, unless, unless, something personal came into his daily routine. In this case Stanford broke into that very routine. That was the problem, he had chaffed at the blatant unruliness of the hippies – losers, as he had called them on occasion - and he thought they, by sheer numbers, had taking advantage of the 'live and let live' attitude in Bolinas, this included Hollywood, who was living on the beach and building these monumental sculptures. "There was a liability issue," he thought, "and ultimately he could be called on the carpet for allowing Hollywood to continue." But he had closed his eyes to it as long as the payoffs kept coming – it was a simple case of an emerging cultural co-dependence…" When Stanford contacted him after he found the scarf hanging on the metal guitar player Roderick's thoughts turned to the possibility that there might be something serious in Stanford's charges. "This time the flagrant drunk would have to be worked over."

"Are you sure it's your wife's scarf?" he questioned Stanford after they finally found seats at Mariah's.

"Listen, I would know it, of course it's hers, it was hanging on that monstrosity…"

"All right, all right, how long did you say she's been gone?"

"She left about five weeks ago, I've been staying at Smileys for the last week, hoping there would be some news. With all the things going on around here, I thought maybe she would show up here. It was a long shot, I was ready to give up, now I don't know what to think…"

"Maybe she was here and she gave him the scarf."

Stanford just shook his head.

"Maybe, he simply found it on the beach, like he said."

"Well, he acted strange when I wanted it. He didn't want me to have it. I had to tear the thing down."

"And…"

"Well, there were a lot of so called hippies out there who were ready to lynch me when I confronted the guy."

"So much for peace, eh? He's become an icon for them, one of the free souls, from the land…"

"As far as I'm concerned he knows something, she was obviously here. How else did her scarf get there?"

"We'll have to find out."

"There was someone with me last night, a man named Schilling who's also staying at Smileys. Interestingly, he's doing research on the hippie phenomenon. He'll vouch for what happened."

"So, fill me in."

"Well, I had walked the beach with Schilling looking for Julia, showing her picture to people hanging out, even some guru who was holding court on the other side."

"That's not news around here."

"He goes by Shiva, white robe, long hair, some of those people called him the new messiah. That night they were branding themselves. It was bizarre. I felt like I had come into some religious revival meeting expecting to hear people speaking in tongues, or I had dropped into some tribal drug ritual…"

"I've met the guy. At the time I thought he was another stoked up hippie."

"He's got quite the charisma, kids were flocking around him. We talked to him, had quite a conversation. I showed him Julia's photo…"

"And?"

"He said he hadn't seen her but…"

"But what?"

"He seemed vague."

"Let's take one thing at a time, shall we, first I'll pay a visit to Hollywood."

"I would like to go along. If he's had anything to do with Julia…?"

"There is still the law, we do have due process here."

"Of course, but something happened to her…"

By this time Mariah had eavesdropped enough to ask Roderick what brought him to Bolinas? Something about Hollywood?"

"We just wanna ask him some questions."

"About what?"

"Business…"

"What's he done now?"

"The usual."

"Give him a break, Roderick, he cleans up the beach."

"That may be the problem."

"What do you mean?"

"Look, I don't know."

Stanford could not hold back. "Look, he had my wife's scarf on one of his metal things."

"And…"

She's been missing for five weeks."

There was a silence. Mariah seemed to put the situation into a context she understood. Her eyes rolled. "Mmm…" was all the response she would give.

135

"Look, she's gone, something happened to her and he's got her scarf, OK, so what do you think?"

"Stanford, I think that's enough for now. Mariah we'll take the bill."

At this point both Mariah and Stanford were visibly agitated. She was no fan of Roderick's but they had tolerated each other. By letting him have the occasional coffee on the house when he came into town he ignored the usual bureaucratic infractions. "Live and let live," he had told her, "as long as nothing bites me in the ass." That was basically his philosophy on the beat around Marin. Mariah's place was no different but when it came to possible manslaughter, as in this case, he took an official position.

"I'm going to get Schilling," Stanford said as they departed, "He'll corroborate the whole story...and I have the scarf..."

At this point Mariah had also heard enough to feel her sense of motherly protection rising up. She had had her difficulties with Hollywood but he had become part of the extended family, part of the village. She wasn't going to let one of her own be accused of some phony rap. "No way," she thought, "I'm going to bring a few people into this." She left the place to Josh who usually took his breaks from the Shoppe and hung out at her place.

On her way past the General Store she thought of the conversation and her relationship with Hollywood. She had nursed him on several occasions, knew the extent of his vulnerability and his anger. "That's why he drinks for god's sakes," she said out loud as she went by the garage picking up her pace. "He's helped me out, damn it." She said, getting more worked up thinking about this slick preppy accusing him of what: having something to do with this long lost woman. By this time she had turned the corner and was heading to the Grandiose. "Somebody's gotta back him up." She thought and turned down the driveway..."Val!" she yelled out, "Nancy, are you back there?" She looked through the over grown blackberry bushes towards the back of the lot. The ram shackle shack that they lived in was dark. Light and conversation was coming out of the kitchen in the hotel. "Val..." she called out as she went through the back door and into the kitchen where a number of people were sitting around the table.

"Where is Val?" She inquired.

Shoulders shrugged, Damian was sipping peppermint tea with his new girl friend and told her he had seen Val in the store. Seeing how agitated she was, he asked her what was wrong.

"Jesus, she responded, "that guy lookin for his wife is accusing Hollywood of having something to do with her..."

Her outburst brought everyone within earshot to attention.

"What did he have to do with her?" someone said.

The questions continued until Mariah finally said, "I think he might need some support."

"Yea, sure..."

Before too long the commotion had gone up the stairs. Someone had

136

told Jane, who let Shiva and Marshall know. By the time Marshall came down Mariah had a number of people around her, including Damian, who were going to accompany her to the hogan on the beach.

"Is Shiva here?" she asked.

By this time a figure stood in the portal of the stairs leading to the rooms. As each follower gazed on the white robed man the room quieted and a sense of calm pervaded, smiles grew on their faces. His hair was glowing from the backlight of the staircase, his robe was shining from the kitchen light, only his face was strangely shadowed. He was looking but his eyes were lowered…

"Shiva, " Mariah dared to break the silence. She still related to him as she had the first day he was in the café with Sweet. "Shiva, Hollywood is being accused of abducting this missing woman. We're going to give him some support. Can you help?"

He stood there, immobilized, until the kitchen occupants began to feel uneasy. They were used to his thoughtful hesitations but this seemed like a simple request and they thought he would respond much quicker.

Finally, he said, in an unusually quiet voice, "Life has its reasons. Not every action is understood. Choose your time to respond, to act, and to react to the outside world. Let go of that which keeps you from being in the moment…Go in peace…"

With his quiet exhortation, most of the followers nodded their heads but Mariah was not so easily dissuaded from doing more. "I think we should go see Hollywood, let him know we support him…and I, for one, am going…" She stood up and started to walk through the door to the used store…Several others followed her…At this point Shiva, his eyes downcast, not really looking at who or what, quietly reiterated his position, "Go in peace…"

30

Free Hollywood

Mariah's movement was edgy, shifting from the uneven, root infested sidewalk to the street. Several visitors had joined her, gesticulating and attracting others. When the small crowd turned the corner onto Main Street they saw a police car leave the front of Scowleys heading towards the lagoon. Mariah urged them to pick up the pace...

"What's happening?" could be heard in front of the General Store.

"The fuzz is going to hassle Hollywood." Some one said.

"What's he done this time?"

"Something about a missing woman..."

"Look," Mariah said to several rainbow people within earshot, "it looks like our deputy sheriff is going to arrest Hollywood for something he didn't have anything to with..."

"What do you mean?"

"Well, this guy found a scarf on one of Hollywood's musicians and he thinks he had something to do with this woman's disappearance."

"Come on..."

"Yea..."

"Man, Hollywood gets everything off the beach."

"That's just it, isn't it," Mariah answered, "Every time something is missing on the beach Hollywood is blamed for it. It's about time we showed him our support."

When the rag tag crowd came to the café, Mariah walked in to tell Josh she would be a while, "Keep the soup hot," she said, "I think we're gonna need it but if you have to go, close up…"

By this time the swinging doors at Smileys had let several hardnosed drinkers out. Bear was one of them. Sidekick joined them and immediately let out a howl, "Woheeee, it's a riot…"

"A riot," Bear shrugged and laughed, "more like a soup line."

"I don't know, Bear, they're up to something."

"Well, let's see what's going on."

The crowd, however, was not waiting for the denizens of Smileys, or anyone else, to continue on their quest. They turned the corner only to be met by a stench of seaweed permeating the street. Out of a hovel of flotsam came the voice of the oracle, "It's an ill wind that blows…" She was in the middle of the street, as if she had been waiting for the strings in the hands of the fates to be unraveled. Now, here, she was met by an accumulation of excited and determined souls who, somehow, had been intertwined into one movement… "It's an ill wind that blows," she repeated.

"You're right," someone called out loud enough to be heard above the din, "and this time it's directed toward the pig in the cruiser."

But the 'pig' in this case was not concerned with a prognostication of *ill winds;* in fact, Roderick had driven his cruiser to the end of Wharf Road, by the breakwater boulders, overlooking the outgoing tide. He and Stanford and Schilling had gotten out and were walking towards the strangely quiet band. For once, no wind, ill or otherwise, was tinkling the abalone…and no drumming was setting the sand in motion. Stanford had the brown and gold woven scarf in his hand, clutching it like some ticket to a secret ritual, where all would be revealed if they asked the right questions and Julia would somehow reappear…

"Hollywood, are you in there?"

Roderick's official voice spread over the beach. The question had been directed towards the hogan next to the broken down pieces of the guitarist. Some traces of blood were still seen on the dry parts of the beach. A number of people had already gathered around Roderick the authority, wondering what the fuss was about, but there was no sound coming from the hogan.

"Hollywood," Roderick stated again, "I want to talk to you."

No answer.

He walked up to the entrance, moved the blanket over the entry and looked in. His eyes squinted trying to look around…Without warning he heard Hollywood's voice, "My grandfather once said, If you wait long enough the world will come to your door."

"I'm not the world, Hollywood, I'm not even the President. I'm just the

140

deputy sheriff and I want to ask you about the scarf you found." He stepped back to let Hollywood come out.

"I'll tell you like I told the guy that punched me, I found it on the beach."

"When?"

"Some days ago."

"Was there anything else with it?"

By this time Stanford and Schilling had come to the interrogation. After them came a number of beachcombers and hippies and curious bystanders. Roderick was finding it a bit stifling and lacking in official demeanor. It got to a point where he finally asked Hollywood to accompany him to his cruiser. Hollywood, at first hesitated, but Roderick took him by the arm and began to lead him to it with the strange entourage following them. When they reached the cruiser another crowd was coming down the street to meet them. Animated by the sight of Hollywood being taken into the car someone shouted, "Free Hollywood!"

"Yea, free Hollywood…" someone else repeated.

It wasn't what Roderick had expected or, for that matter, Hollywood, who was by now in the cruiser and sat rather stoically thinking about what his grandfather would have said. For once he couldn't come up with a quick saying, but maybe, he thought, the world was coming to his door, maybe that's all he needed, maybe he would get noticed… the possibility couldn't hurt…

Roderick, however, was not looking for publicity. He was not in the mood for explaining things to anybody let alone a bunch of dope heads. "Jesus, Stanford, it looks like we got ourselves some activity." He finally said. Before Stanford or Schilling could say anything Roderick was walking out in front of the crowd, "What the hell is going on here?" he yelled out trying to show some authority. When he spotted Mariah he looked at her and asked in a questioning tone what the party was all about?

"We are not letting Hollywood out of here…"

"Now, you're not going to have any choice in that Mariah." He could feel his anger rising. I'd suggest you all split up and head on home or wherever you're staying…"

Someone in the crowd lifted a makeshift sign that read *Free Hollywood*. A shout went up when it turned around. *Free Hollywood* became the mantra…*free Hollywood free Hollywood free Hollywood*…Roderick tried to speak through the chanting, "I think you better head on home, I'm taking this guy in, all right, we're just going to talk to him all right," but his words were lost in the name of *Free Hollywood*. In disgust, Roderick turned around and headed back to his cruiser. When he was close enough he realized the cruiser wasn't going anywhere, soon, someone had let the air out of the two front tires. His face began to blend with the crimson on some tie-dyed T-shirts. In his case it was not the color of joy but seething rage. He could hardly speak. His mouth opened but nothing came out. His 'live and let live' attitude had been replaced with an anger he had not felt for a long time. This was not just an official response but had become personal. When his voice finally found the words he yelled

141

out, "Get outta my way, Goddamn it..." He pushed his way to the cruiser's door and hopped in, started it and was ready to back up with two flat tires and Hollywood in the back seat. Stanford and Schilling had moved off to the side and watched with questioning anticipation. The engine revved and he was ready to back up but a number of young people were in the way, some had sat down, others were in the process...He was not going anywhere without running someone down. He revved the motor again hoping to scare them into moving, but instead, more people sat down, all around the cruiser. Someone started chanting again, *free Hollywood...*

Roderick was seething, on the verge of calling headquarters, but he really didn't want them to think he couldn't handle the simple apprehension of a drunk on the beach. The chanting grew, someone started rocking the cruiser, others joined in, the cruiser was rocking and rolling, Roderick was not longer red but his face had turned pale with some sense of fear in his eyes, whether for himself or for others he was not sure – he was being attacked. Stanford shook his head and looked at Schilling, who was thinking, "This is not looking good, He's gonna panic..." Out of anger and fear and an age-old response to defend, Roderick put his hand on his gun, he was not rational at this point, but he was just going to scare them off, he could have called in, he could have let Hollywood go and picked him up later which might have diffused the situation, he could have called in, but instead, he put his hand on his gun, pulled it out, just to scare them and maybe take one shot into the sky, put his hand on the gun, pulled it out and opened the door intending to shoot into the sky but the rockingrolling cruiser and the swaying door would not let him – someone saw the gun and screamed, the car rocked back, the door shut on him on his arm the gun went off the gun went off...screams were heard and the jostling and panicking and moving of bodies became chaotic, the gun had gone off, the cruiser settled down, the screaming quieted, the movement of bodies slowed down to places of refuge and safety, at least far enough away from the gun, until a slight peacefulness descended on the road and beach and lagoon – Roderick was in slow motion, he had not left his seat since the explosion.

Everywhere and everything was relatively still, the crowd had moved away from the cruiser, away from Roderick, that is, everyone but a very still person lying face down in the rough pavement...it looked like a girl in rolled-up jeans and bare feet with a sun-yellow T-shirt, her long straight brown hair was covering her face and a slow oozing deep red color was dying the rough grey pavement around her...

Schilling was the first to react to the surreal quiet. He rushed over to the body and turned her shoulder, her body over...it was soaked in the red of life-oozing blood...There was no more rocking of the cruiser, no more chanting, no more freeing Hollywood, it wouldn't have been necessary, anyway, Hollywood had freed himself...In the ensuing chaos, someone had simply opened the back door of the cruiser and he had walked out. The commotion and the rocking had left him shaken, almost dizzy, as he

142

headed towards his hogan - yet his mind was not on escape but on returning to the scene and rectifying and healing, if he could…

By the time Stanford went to Roderick most of the crowd had realized that something had happened. A number of shocked and saddened young people had drawn closer to their fallen comrade with exclamations rising in disbelief…Another reality was slowly sinking in, Stanford tried to break through to Roderick, get him to call for help, for an ambulance. With Roderick stuttering and in a daze, Stanford realized he would have to attempt it, he reached for the two-way radio, pushed the button, "someone's been shot…" he blurted out, "a girl's hurt, at the end of Wharf Road, just off the beach, the entrance to the beach, we need an ambulance!"

Schilling and several others were huddled over the blood-dyed girl, her eyes glazed, lying in stillness…"Oh my god, its Helen!" someone cried out, "It's Helen, Helen…" Several people, with distressed faces, moved walked closer to her as her friend continued to cry out, "Helen, oh my god, Helen…" She looked in her eyes, kneeled beside her, others came closer, Schilling tried to keep some kind of order but the cries were increasing and the crowd was closing in on the blood red dyed pavement, closing in on the sweet face whose eyes had closed, there was no movement, a peacefulness had descended on her…someone threw a flower, a gesture that was soon followed by more flowers, petals, garlands, a gesture coming out of a need to respond to a terrible finality – no matter how innocent or unintentional this momentary act was, it had changed the world. One act, with the force of an explosion, changed the world, creating a memory out of a vital life throbbing human being, a memory for everyone who had touched her, who had known her…Mariah was one of the few close enough to kneel beside her. Her realization of the consequences of her, now questionable, cause was etched in her face, "Good god," she said over and over, shaking her head…flowers and flower petals had begun to cover the still lifeless body. Mariah and Schilling and her close friends stayed with her while others came and went continuing to shower her with flowers, which grew and rose into a flower pyre. Stanford had stayed with Roderick in the cruiser…waiting…

Hollywood had come back and brought with him sage which he lit to let the smoke waft over her…the time of questioning had passed, his role had changed from possible perpetrator to potential healer, not just of her spirit body but the collective body, the young people who had witnessed the act, the friends who knew her, even the deputy sheriff who was still in shock…In shock, from what? An avoidable accident? Yet a probable possibility, given the situation and the fact that he had a gun. Or was it a destined fate – the unraveling of the strings of destiny, or, should that be relegated to a 19th century Wagnerian opera?

Hollywood spread the healing smoke of the smoldering sage over the innocent young still resting girl and over the kneeling friends and those who had come when the tragic word had spread. In that encircling smoke, in that smudging of healing smoke, something happened to

Stanford. He saw the man, holding the sage, in a different way, this time he looked into his eyes, surrounded by the chiseled reminder of a thousand generations lived in the sun, he saw a man whose calm and purposeful presence seemed to change the mood of the crowd...As he sat next to Roderick, he felt something in himself change also, a change towards Hollywood. His animosity left him and a respect penetrated his feelings for the man he had hit – this was not the man who had or would harm his wife. For the first time he believed him. With this recognition, his heavy heart let go of Julia while at the same time he let go of revenge – but it was not for long- the presence of Roderick reminded him of the terrible life-changing event that had occurred, that he was now a party to the death of a young woman who had not just disappeared but was lying in the midst of anguish and flowers, slowly his lightness grew heavier and he realized that from now on he would also be living with this reality, his eyes closed...was there no way out?

The siren stopped and the crowd parted. Another reality entered which would turn the questions upside down and the girl would be objectively treated by outside trained personnel – eventually the sheriff came to coordinate the investigation and at some point the tow truck came to pump up the tires of the cruiser...

Mariah had stayed with the fallen angel until the emergency crew raised her up and carried her away, leaving a flower bed with the soft shape of what was Helen within it, a flower bed for a flower child, she thought, as she walked away and back to her café. She didn't know how to feel, she walked in a daze, seeing others yet not seeing, even touching yet not touching those who were lingering. All was dream like, the mesa the lagoon, Wharf Road, all was dreamlike until a harsh singing voice called her, "Mariiiiiii ah..." She heard it but it was out of some other world, "Mariah blows the stars around...and sets the clouds a flyin, Mariah makes the mountains sound like folks was up there dying...Mariiiiiii ah... Mariiiiii ah...like folks was up there dying..." the voice cracked and crackled attempting that song...Had she seen the Broadway musical? The voice came from the flotsam that moved to join Mariah's slow dreamlike walk back to Scowleys, back to her sanctuary, back to what she knew...

"This isn't the time for corny songs," is all Mariah could muster up in response. But the oracle was not through. It dogged her and goaded her until she thought to herself, "Get a hold of yourself, kid. A young life has been snuffed out...and if she was a Buddhist she could be paying for past sins but since I don't believe in reincarnation this random senseless accidental act turns into the end for a young girl on the cusp of living. I don't understand it...I don't want to understand it...

"Get the hell back into the mud!" she suddenly yelled at the shadowed phantom of flotsam next to her, "I hate your goddamned indifference, as if nothing mattered..." she stopped, her eyes closed...quietly saying to herself, "as if it was all the same..."

Here we go again...bear with me dear patient reader, I am consumed...

It's 6 in the morning and I've been swimming in her death, her dying also. I didn't expect it I didn't expect this scenario it could have been different the event could have been different any event any event could have occurred but it was this one this one I didn't even know her I don't know her I don't know this Helen. Who is she? How well do her friends know her? Are they going to let her parents know? And what are her parents going to think? Will they be ecstatic? What kind of a bullshit comment is that...This child, probably born in 1950, brought up by mother father who knows but all of their 16 years and all of her 16 years ended up in Bolinas not even on the beach but on the rough pavement of Wharf Road on the rough pavement it could have happened differently Roderick could have pulled out his gun gotten out shot in the air and the whole thing could have ended right there or at least changed the noise of his gun could also have brought down the eroding cliff and the gazebo on top of Hollywood's hogan on top of the other musicians 'the music could have died' right there or Roderick could have panicked and driven back and over some one...But all of that or any of that was not to be what was to be was like any other act event happening actuality it just was to be and when any acteventhappeningactuality comes into existence none other could have happened prediction is based on events that have happened with a good probability of them happening again the sun rising yet...yet it never rises the same way with the same stream of light and heat Schrödinger's cat became a philosophical reality Schrödinger's Helen...Helen who launched a strange requiem...became a literate reality Helen named by her parents born sometime after the great war Helen became a reality and her death and her friends and Roderick and everyone in that moment of dying and death changed with her...

I'm not angry with this! It's almost a release and I recognize it, now that I have had a close friend die, I have seen a release of the life forces and I have experienced it and it can be beautiful a slow beauty of ebbing life forces...if death is slow...

But death can also be a purging of the inner angst of the id or flailing frustration...Suddenly! Like a slap by an iterant monk, I understand sacrifice...Tarkovsky recognized it and attempted to portray it in his film Sacrifice...Jesus becoming the Christ Jesus Christ who are you what have you sacrificed? Lloyd Weber, too, asked the question. Was Jesus just a victim caught in his victim hood? Or was his death a death that became the Balm of Gilead for millions of others through his sacrifice? Did he orchestrate it? Did he really want it? Did he take it on because he understood what sacrifice meant for human beings aware of suffering and death? And, it did not end there...sacrifice was not enough, purging was not enough, something beyond sacrifice was needed...a glorious resurrection was needed and conceived for all strugglinghurtingpained despairingangstridden human beings...

But I see on Wharf Road that the resurrection was not a glorious event conceived and painted by Raphael but simply and profoundly a changing of hearts and minds affected by that event. A changing in their lives, a fulcrum that brought about movement and change in their lives…

31

Descent into Darkness

At the Grandiose Hotel, there was no intimation of a young girl's accidental death. All concern seemed to be on interpersonal relationships as Shiva ascended the stairs again, with Marshall following him, wanting to continue their earlier conversation. Hollywood was not Marshall's concern. It was Shiva he had confronted and wanted to engage. He felt he had only begun to mine the truth of their relationship, that his enlightenment would come through personal interaction, with someone he could lean against, push, if he had to, someone who was inwardly strong enough to endure the total angst he had felt in his life… Shiva had been there…had shaken him to his core…

When they entered the room of revelation, Shiva's thoughts, again, turned inward, in a way that not even he fully understood or could avoid, at least not with his usual ability to separate between what was on his mind and people acting on him. "Who was this man, Marshall, to confront him with that intensity of being?" he frustratingly questioned, remembering Marshall's eyes burning through him. Had he not been able to stay one step above this, to stay in his own inner world while the outer world worked its way around him? Had he not also been able to unify and intertwine the polarity of his inner being; the yin and yang aspects; the extreme forces; those subconscious hallucinations, painful, as they were, that he had experienced in the reflections of those revealing windowpanes. Was there any reconciliation possible? Could he find some unifying synthesis for these conflicts? Finally, he had come to the stripped bare bones crux of his question: How could he reconcile the outward saint or master or ecstatic medium and the person who had let another human being die? That was it wasn't it? He had let another human being die - just let her walk to her death...and, and not be truthful in his part in it, the cause of her death. Was this reminder to become his descent into darkness, his long day's trip into night?

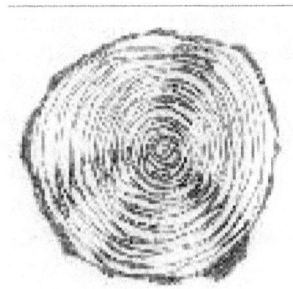

32

A Few Rare People

"The cause of her death," he repeated, while very vague images began to reveal themselves on the glass. They were fortunately vague, for his own sanity, because one image was closer to his child hood fears - something out of *Dr. Jekyll and Mr. Hyde*. Or something out of *Forbidden Planet*, where the force of evil was a grotesquely energized accumulation of primal subconsciousness – the id – so aptly named by Freud.

Was this his subconscious evil side or was this a 19th century phenomenon? Was it an earlier Christian based dichotomy? Surely he had gone beyond that, yet there it was, a grotesque image of evil. Where was the good? What were these simplistic terms to him? They were for the ignorant, fearful believers who usually made a joke out of intellectual development. Was there anything new to add to these extremes of human behavior? Was this just one more set up for his moral ambivalence? And why wasn't moral ambivalence considered a paradigm of human behavior? No! Too, too often moral ambivalence had been dismissed by those who see in black and white, showing the grotesque in contrast to the beauty…But the darkness only drove him deeper into his thoughts, "Who lives by these extremes? Who can unify these extremes without falling into the grip or mental security of one side or the other?" he asked himself almost out loud, "A few rare people? A...few...rare...people?"

For a moment he was alone, yes, there were others around but he was alone in his thoughts and they knew him well enough, by now, to leave him in this somnambulistic state with his eyelids twitching and his body slowly rocking back and forth, his arms folded in front of him with his right hand propping up his chin. Slowly he rocked, his thoughts on moral behavior and the cultural history of moral behavior...realizing, he, too, could never fully extract himself from his own behavior. "Where, in fact, did conscience come from?" he thought, "When did a consciousness of wrong and right come into human consideration? During the long history of human interaction, when did the first instances, the first realizations of a wrongful act come into our conscious thinking?"

This was the epitome of his inner struggle. He was trying to understand his situation within an abstract historical context and, he thought, it might illuminate the dilemma but, he also felt, it would not ultimately define it. At one time, for example, survival was so close to each individual and to family life that the larger extended family took on the survival values and ethics of the basic family unit, every one lived for the survival of the group. Over thousands of years these patterns of behavior evolved and developed into cultural ethics, mores and rituals.

He recalled meeting a woman while he was singing on a corner, in Salt Lake City, no less. She had listened to his words on a Main Street corner in the shadow of the Mormon Temple,

The rulers of mediocrity
Can darken the world that you see
And close off the joy that can be
If you go too far you'll see
They will detain you
They will restrain you
They will then chain you
To the weight of all of their fears
Like vultures with blood in the air
That circle and live in despair
And dive for the beauty that's rare
If you stay too long you'll see
They will then tear you
They'll strip and then bear you
Then they will swear that
They're doing all for your very own good

With the angel Moroni blowing his trumpet on the spire of the temple he sang,

Ten thousand years of pain
Does it have to happen again?
They put another joyful man in chains

150

If you spread your arms you'll see
They will not heed you
They will just bleed you
They will feed you to a page of tragedy
Radiant one
Can it be can it be?
Radiant one
Can it be can it be?
That no one can live with what you've become
That no one can live with what you've become
Beautiful hands
Don't they see don't they see
That you have achieved what they could become
That you have achieved what they could become
Radiant sun
In your face in your eyes
Light the way light my eyes
Radiant one
Radiant one

She came up to him as the words slowly faded into the Mormon past and at the same time reflected the Mormon present – the administrative building towering over the temple. The business of organized religion is big business as Francis of Assisi found out hundreds of years ago when he presented himself to the pope. The contrast between his humble faith and the opulence of the Vatican was beautifully contrasted in the film *Brother Sun Sister Moon*. A man of simple faith and love is seen walking up, what seems like, an eternal, grand staircase, to meet the apex of the Pope's religious decorative magnificence. The dogma of organized religion is also not to be questioned, as Galileo found out 500 years ago, when the pope forbade him from teaching his ideas; among them was the heretical idea that the earth might not be the center of the universe. Galileo was allowed to live if he recanted, which he did and as a result was allowed to live in isolation with his knowledge, not knowing that he would eventually be vindicated. Today the answer for a faith based understanding of the world for so many so-called intelligent people is: If you don't understand our strange, often contradictory beliefs don't worry, don't tax your mental abilities with them, God, Allah, Jehovah, etc will eventually clear it all up – use your intelligence to add numbers, check your portfolio, buy a new Chevy or any of a million things that will keep your mind occupied, you just have to have faith...

Most of these, relatively benign believers, however, are just another unfortunate thorn in the side of a thoughtful and intelligent understanding of contemporary life on the planet. But compare these to the true believers belonging to a more insidious and horrific group – the religious fanatics and other ideological fanatics and extremists who would change the very basis of human civilization and its core values with grotesque acts of terror and then justify their horror by believing they will gain in

151

some after-life…or even gain something in this life. There is no comparison. And for those who think technological terrorism through horrendous destruction is justified without ever seeing the eyes of a ripped apart child, to think that just because we don't see the eyes of that ripped apart bloody child it is all right to technologically destroy. There is no comparison…

"Your song gives me this generalized impression." She said after I had finished singing and the strings had ceased to vibrate, "about something Carl Jung called an archetype." I was fascinated by her comment. She was older and invited me to her home to talk some more. She wanted me to look at Jung's book *Man and His Symbols*. I went a few days later and it was one of those evenings that I will never forget, when my vague questions were evaluated in the light of Carl Jung's life work – a man who thought deeply about human imagination and the symbolic extensions imbedded in our cultural achievements. He made me think about this fertile field of human activity out of which evolved physical symbols - imbued with meaning; physical objects combined with human imagination and consciousness - symbols adding values to our lives, the accumulated expressions of our 10,000 years of beliefs. To transform them we must include them as part of our history. Each of us must include the world's symbols as our own. We must imagine ourselves looking at the earth from space. We are all human beings within the environment of the earth – the living breathing earth…our various beliefs and their various symbols are to be appreciated as the imaginative expressions of our cultural history…

In this way, at this time, we are all of our past, all of our ingrained expressions of our past – we are all religious expressions – Moslem, Jewish, Buddhist, Christian, Jain, Hindu, Confucius on and on – we are all of these. If you are asked what is your religion, tell them you are all religions, even better, tell them you are the kernel of truth in all religions – you are the archetype of religion, even the archetype of ideology…

His mind was reeling from his solitary discourses. He cried out: *Marshall!* and Marshall answered, "Shiva, what, what is it? I'm here, we are all here…listening…"

But Shiva had exhausted himself. At this point it was air he needed, more than thoughts or images, more that the novelty of the worm gear apparatus, it was the moist cooling invigorating air wafting in from the great expanse of evaporative ocean he needed. He held onto to the window sill and slowly sank to his knees, the windows were open wide enough to let him breathe and he filled his lungs to the fullest as if there were no breath left, as if it was his last…finally breathing out, he could only hold it for so long…mmmmmmmmmmmm mmmmmmmmmmmmmmmmmmmm…air filled, intoxicated, high on the anima of earthly creation, the thin very thin layer of earthly atmosphere, of circulating atoms…He breathed in and out until his eyes opened ever so slightly, just enough to vaguely see movement in the glass, the windows of his earlier discoveries his inner world reflected in the panes of the outside, vague images becoming clarified, edges of marble columns becoming fluted and hard to the touch, his fingers following the edges upward now down…

"Just as this marble is hard to the touch and as it was transformed by the hands and tools of those trained artisans who carved out the flutes to add beauty to this age-old stone – just as they added meaning to this stone we are here to add meaning to our actions…" His toga, weathered, worn, hung on him like his words hung on to me. I'd heard him speak, or question more than speak, over the years, ever since I was taken from Persia, kept alive, a slave to Pericles, citizen of Athens. When peace came and I was freed I had been to the agora many times, listened to the discourses on freedom and now, here, I was free to go but did not want to. I felt myself a living example of their discussions on freedom…they were free citizens of Athens; I had been a slave and was now free. And what was that? I had changed. Should I go back to Persia? I could not. Something held me here. What was the freedom in that? I was not free. In my mind I was not free. I would never be free of the ideas I had heard them discuss, or free of their banter, their questioning – that is it, more than anything – their questioning. I never questioned the place I came from, my family or my traditions until I was uprooted, violently uprooted, *I was lucky to be alive* he heard a local singer sing. Standing under the shade of the covered market, I felt more than lucky, I felt privileged to be among those questioning citizens. There was one who seemed to be relentless in his questioning, not only of local customs, but also of the leaders of Athens and also, their gods. He always brought about, or should I say, stirred a lively interchange.

"At some point our actions take on meaning, and this is what we must consider."

Someone in the crowd responded that meaning comes out of each family and clan and ancestors – it is what and how they add to the meaning."

"So meaning is handed down, in addition to our actions, and is told by the elders and grandfathers and grandmothers and story tellers to the next generation?"

"Eventually, it becomes the larger community - becomes Athens - becomes Sparta?"

"Meaning becomes the values we live by, becomes the procession to Athena every four years, with the robe woven by the virgins. It takes on homage to the gods as well as establishing ways to settle disputes in the market place."

"These values can also become codified and rigid. There is the danger."

"And what is the danger, if they show us the right way to live?"

Again, Socrates emphasized the direction of the discussion,

"That is the question to pursue. Are we living right?

"If we are, our values should coincide with our community. If we are not living right and the gods show their wrath, how do our values change to correct the way we live?"

"Exactly, how, then, do our values change?"

"They change from within."

"Yet, the influence can come from outside of us?"

"From outside of our community, outside of Athens."

"From outside of our confederation."

"There is no outside. Zeus watches over our lives."

"Even the heathen?"

"They are not of us, yet they are."

"They are not citizens of Athens."

At this point a frustrated man, who had been listening to the back and forth discussion, turned to Socrates and, in a blaring voice, said, "Why do you keep questioning our values."

Socrates, just as forcefully, replied, "To get to the truth!"

"Our values are true, therefore they are the truth!"

"Without question?"

"Without question."

"Then you will permit me to make a statement."

"Yes."

"Sparta's values are true for the Spartans, are they also true of the Athenians?"

"You said a statement, not a question."

"Then you would agree with the statement that Sparta's values are true."

"You are still asking a question."

He smiled, "Yes, I am. I thought I could entice you into examining your beliefs."

"I am quite aware of that."

"Yet you were not persuaded. Why is that?"

"I do not question what is true."

"What you are saying is that there is an absolute truth."

"I did not say that."

"You said, you did not question what is true."

"Yes."

"What is true, then?"

"What I believe; what has been passed on to us; what the citizens of Athens accept as true."

"Spartans believe that boys should be taken from their mothers when they are six years old in order to become warriors of Sparta. Is this a belief you agree with?"

"Spartans have their own beliefs about how to educate their boys. Athenians think that boys should stay at home until they are old enough to be educated by their teachers into the arts – such as oratory, to be initiated into the physical and intellectual and artistic arts until they are ready to take on the role of citizen."

"You said Spartans have their own beliefs. You would then agree that Athenians and Spartans have different beliefs?"

"Their beliefs are different but they arise out of the same truth."

"So, there is one truth. Tell me then, if the results or beliefs arising out of the same truth are different how can you tell when beliefs are just beliefs and when they are a fixed truth?"

"You cannot tell."

"Does it matter if you can not tell?"

"We accept Sparta's beliefs and live our beliefs."

"Because they both arise out of a universal truth."

"Yes…"

As he said this Socrates realized how quiet the market place had become. It was evening and the air was beginning to cool. A number of other toga-clad citizens had been listening to the exchange including a young man who had been writing on a slate. Socrates took the momentary lull to ask him his name, "Plato," he replied.

"And what have you been writing on your slate?"

"Your discourse on 'truth'," he responded.

"Do you think it will have any meaning outside of here, Plato?"

Before he could answer the market place grew darker, the columns and buildings of the agora threw shadows on the side of the Acropolis. He had been there in vivid remembrance but the discussion on truth had only allowed Shiva a momentary respite from the shadows now growing more ominous and darker…he was not ready for shadows, did not want to take in the other side. His mind struggled to stay in the light but it was no use, he was caught in his own conscience of right and wrong, what was true in this? He wanted to cry out…but from some deep hidden place a voice spoke to him like a commentator out of some documentary, "…and they devised methods to extend the pain without a man passing out or losing consciousness; that would only reduce their sense of power, for it was this infliction of pain on another human being that gave them their power, their momentary power and it was this forever horror of pain in every imaginable cruel infliction that made those inflicting the pain think they were stronger – stronger than human weakness, stronger than empathy, stronger than the possibility of love. They loathed the weak groveling of human beings and, yet, they groveled in their own self-righteous creating reasons for the infliction of these horrors. They could not be could not would not could not feel…now, here, we see one warped inhuman human being feeling incredibly powerful as he takes the red hot sharpened steel pointed spear in his hand. In the cruel dripping dank darkness, lit by the fire light, illuminating every sharp edge of rock and stone, the fire, now, was coming home in all its bright beauty, the white hot steel was slowly brought into the gaze of desperate eyes. This fragile flesh bound human being with the desperate eyes felt the heat as his outstretched arms stretched, as he was stretched from a rope that was pulled through a pulley high in the ceiling of this black pit. A cruel warped inhuman outrage held the white hot sharpened point up and put the other end into a pit in the floor, someone lowered the dangling mass of a man spreading his legs, lowering this once confident man down until he felt the heat between his legs, lowering this soft fleshy feeling man down until the white hot point ripped and burned its way into his ass hole slowly they did not want him to pass out slowly aaaaaaaaaaaaa

155

aaaaaaaaaaaaaaaaaaa the horrific wailing crying screaming coming from the mouths of a thousand tortured human beings was music to the ears of this horribilishuman momentarily or forever separated from feeling and emotion and empathy and compassion and love...this nonhumanhuman was inflicting the pain and letting the weight of this so-called blasphemer, this human being who had done nothing but believe in his own simple way, who had done nothing but live in shades of brown or black or red or yellow or white who had done nothing but be brought down to that dehumanized and marginalized and horribly named and symbolized state...they let the weight of this every innocent human being slowly push the red hot steel deeper into his soft guts his intestines running with blood aaaaaaaaaaaaa aaaaaaaaaaaaaaaaaaaa it went until... Was it a shot? Was it a rock? Was it his fist striking the glass? A blow that shattered the glass, the pane, his fists, his knuckles bleeding, his face in contortions of misery and despair, his hands bleeding, blood dripping on his white robe, he was not sure where he was his eyes barely able to see through his anguish. I am not what you think I am he yelled in a voice reduced to guttural sounds and sobs. I am not what you think I am he yelled again as he turned and ran through the horrified gaping followers, his robe spotted with blood, his face in furrows his body in convulsions...He threw himself down the stairs. I cannot be what you want me to be. I am no Christ on the cross. He ran through the kitchen, past the washer and dryer, out the back door, down the alley, onto the street, through the waiting crowd, past the VW van. I am no Christ, there is no salvation, his words convulsing through his agony. I am not who you think I am I am...his cries fading as he ran past Mesa Street, as he ran into the darkness, the lagoon on his right, as he ran into the shadowed darkness of the eucalyptus tunnel his red blood and white robe reduced to grays and black and yet someone said years later they thought they saw light moving through the narrow road surrounded caved by eucalyptus trees *I am not what you think I am I am fading away I am...*

33

I Think He's Flown

The west-facing room of the Grandiose Hotel had turned strangely quiet and any residual creaking on the steps had settled.   All who had witnessed the frantic bloodied state of Shiva and the shattering of the glass, the crystalnacht of his soul, were in abeyance. The windows that had illuminated untold unknown inner struggles were haphazardly and sharply spread on the old worn wool carpet. Through hallucinations of on one kind or another these panes had bared his soul and ripped the skin off his routine reality. The half filled half full destiny that he had almost consummated, did not have an historical ending – known and embellished and contemplated. There was no burning at the stake or crucifixion on the mesa, no commemoration in oils or tempura or murals, no, his was a run for survival at any cost…

Marshall was the first to recognize the gravity of the situation. Looking around, his eyes found Jane's. They looked into each other until he asked, "What the hell was that about?"

Jane, looking incredulous, said, "Let's go." and motioned for them to follow the trail of blood. Others, who had quietly come into the room while

Shiva was ruminating, gathered themselves, stood up and followed. On the road they found two or three drops of blood, no more. They assumed he went in the direction of the mesa and turned onto Mesa Road, not noticing the vague frantic hell bent figure actually running north along the lagoon, running north into a tunnel of Eucalyptus trees, running north into anonymity…

"This is crazy!" Jane exclaimed, for anyone to hear. They had walked as far as the fire station. Bright moonlight had gone in and out of the occasional moving night clouds and mist. "This is crazy," she repeated, "Where has he gone?"

Marshall ventured to speak, "I think he's flown…"

34

Sunburst

Several days had passed without word of Shiva. Rumors filled the void, until a young man with an unusually serene countenance walked into the kitchen of the Grandiose. Like a passenger pigeon with a message, he was welcomed by the waiting followers and pulled into the fold by his arms and loose clothes.

"I tried to talk to someone," he told them, "He had shoulder length hair and an intense gaze came from his weathered face. He was sitting on the cliff near Shelter Cove. It was just a happenstance, no more, but he struck me with curiosity. I remember saying 'peace, brother' and he just sat there. After a while I heard him mumble something. I could barely make it out, *I am the earth re re something, I am the earth re…*

When Sweet heard those words, she filled with emotion, she could not hold back, the door opened to her tears. "He's the only one who would know that," she cried. Her anger at his leaving immediately turned into a longing for him, the cool guy she remembered meeting on the mountain highway, the vibes she had felt when they sang Bobby McGee, and later, when they shared the overwhelming experience on the folds of the princess. All this welled up inside her when she heard the words. She knew the ending, she knew it was Shiva, she knew the agony he was experiencing, she knew what he had left and was now soul searching on some lost coast highway somewhere...

"What did he look like?" someone else asked the messenger.

"His long hair was disheveled, he had on worn out dungarees with this white shirt popping out, loose, like straw."

Everyone listened intently, everyone who had witnessed that last evening in that sacred room above the used books and used clutter, in that west-facing room, that literal *window to the soul* that Shiva looked out of and more importantly, unknowingly had gone into. Everyone who had listened to his cultural insights, or epistles, as some had called them, were now sure of the sighting of their master. Each had their own inner relationship with him and felt a mixture of emotions. Jane reiterated her clarion call to them, "He is living. We've got to continue to spread his message of the ecstatic life."

"Jane," Damian responded, "His words are living in me. They won't leave me...what he opened up in me won't leave me..."

Marshall was hesitant. His anger at Shiva's leaving had smoldered for days. He could not reconcile another loss. His needs seemed to require the immediacy of the relationship he had with Shiva, the emotional and physical closeness, the sometimes sparring and sometimes wallowing in their immediacy. Words were not enough for him. Here, again, he challenged those around him as he had Shiva and as he, now, did Jane. Her single-minded pursuit bothered him to the point of confronting her and it was the messenger who facilitated their differences, better yet, who helped them encounter their differences. Eden, as he came to be known, was cognizant of something unusual, even significant, that had occurred here. Each one that he met had their story to tell. In his own way, from his own path he, too, had been looking for some community to fill with his own philosophy culled from the writings of Lao Tzu and Meister Elkhart, as Shiva had before him. Eden was also influenced by Rumi, the Persian poet and others who had immersed themselves in the passion of life`.

Ultimately, Marshall was not persuaded to join the caravan of spiritual disseminators, seekers, thespians, clowns and other ecstatic followers that Sunburst had gathered around her. His experience of the branding and physical pain as an initiation rite had been a point of contention, not just with Sunburst but also with Shiva, who had not endorsed his act or the others who had followed in his wake. "An ecstatic state was within our human potential to fulfill without desecrating the body." That was Shiva's answer to Marshall's branding. "Our ecstatic state is a natural fulfillment of our evolution. It is not a destructive one, either inside or outside of the body."

Sunburst had taken Shiva's side and in a rigid posture stood up to Marshall. He could feel her intransigent intensity; in fact, he could only remember one time before this that she had positioned herself this way -

it was when she had taken on the name of Sunburst, the time she told him and several others the story.

"It was one of those mornings, a few days after I had arrived in Bolinas. I woke up early…I like getting up early, I was thinking about Shiva, his message, thinking about how to get it out into the world, it was early, still foggy over the hills, I was thinking that I've got to take this out and I was thinking about a troupe, a theater troupe, like Julian Beck's *living theater*, going on the road, when the fog over Mount Tam just kind of lifted and opened up and this burst of sunlight came streaming over the top of the mountain - streams of light…It was so magical I thought the sky was exploding, I thought this was meant for me, I thought how am I going to remember this burst of sun. Then I thought I would give myself a new name. I would call myself Sunburst and that's how it happened…

Marshall had sat with an incredulous grin on his face. She sensed that he was not empathetic to her conversion…

"You're laughing at me," she suddenly blurted out. I think you're laughing at me." Her eyes glared, her body tensed. Marshall could feel it. For once he did not want to confront her. "It's a good story, Jane," he said trying to placate her, assuage her, but the psychic damage had been done. She glared at Marshall and several others until her mixture of feelings – frustration, inadequacy, being taken for a fool – all came to a head. " I just think you're not taking me seriously" she said again and walked out on them.

"She'll come back." Someone said.

She did come back. She had already become a force for bringing others into the fold, just as her hopes of a strong spiritual leader had become manifest in Shiva, her vision of a traveling spiritual revival troupe had become more likely with the growth of Shiva's followers. She had this uncanny ability to see the potential in people she met, every one had a story or something they could contribute to the show, whether it was the art of the fantastique with faeries and elves or peace music made by Korean Buddhists. She gathered them to her like some Mother Hubbard. After a while she created her own signposts of the journey by saving tickets, napkins, photos, all manner of objects from her moments with her found people. With these she found time to create collages, in boxes, boards or on canvas, whatever was available?

With Shiva gone she had felt the call, felt the opportunity to fulfill her own dreams, fulfill her own desires, after all, she had left the home of a middle class house wife, she had left, children and a scientist husband behind, she had to find something to replace them…

Marshall pointed his finger at her. "You, you are a witch!"

"Don't you dare talk to me like that!"? She pursed her lips, defiant, immovable.

"You, you just want to use people."

"And you, what do you give them?" she shot back, "You make a big deal out of your encounters, but what do you actually leave them with?"

Taken back, Marshall began to melt in her defiance. Eden was engaged

161

in the whole encounter, almost goading them.

"I'm going to take whoever wants to come along." She finally said. When no answer came from Marshall, she added, "Who ever wants to spread the word."

Eden nodded, others took sides, and some with a burn in their palm edged closed to Marshall. Others asked her when and where?

35

Nostalgia

For Schilling, it was a slow drive back from the sheriff's office. This time the curves seemed relentless and unforgiving. Every blind curve held the possibility of an idiot eyeing the scenery and taking his eyes off the road. He realized it only took a millisecond to cross the line of this narrow two-laner. That would be it, he thought, his life would change dramatically, if he lived. But why continue to think about death, just because a young girl died, just because he had to give his statement concerning the circumstances that brought about her death. Roderick had been taken off duty until the investigation was over. Helen's parents had been notified and they had unfortunately run into Schilling as he was leaving the police station. Their grief shook him even further. He could not construct an easy abstract analysis of those tragic events…

By the time he got back to his room at Smileys he had resolved to see Damian. He wanted to make one more attempt at reconciliation and to tell him that he was going home. As his thoughts dwelled on those words, especially the word *home,* there was an almost nostalgic feeling for his modest cubby hole of a room, not too far from the Fischer Theater in Detroit. It was true that half the room was occupied by his organ and that the rest of the place seemed to be stacked with books and empty beer bottles which were stranded on every remaining flat spot off the floor, yet it was home and he still felt a twinge of homesickness for those surroundings. He wanted to be ensconced at his desk, sorting through his notes, organizing his thoughts, making some sense of this so-called hippie phenomenon, this generational and cultural massage of the mid twentieth century. Something was happening but he didn't know exactly what it was - who were these kids looking for something to protest against, to live for or to die for…and he had seen the tragic results…It was time to pack up but not without paying a visit to the Grandiose to find Damian. He assumed he was still staying there not realizing that

Shiva's self-imposed exile from his followers had left the Grandiose in a strange state of affairs. While the loss of Shiva still allowed them to live together, the schism between Marshall and Jane had created an additional tension in the immediate household. It was an uneasy remembrance, yet, as the word spread of his departure, many had come to pay a kind of homage to the site. Shiva's reputation actually took on a mysterious quality to those who heard the embellished story or stories.

Val didn't mind the extra commotion – many people went through the store and bought something as a memento of the place where the master had lived. The kitchen was crowded with curious visitors, all hoping to take the steps up the narrow staircase to the west-facing room where an alter had been set up and consecrated in front of the window of revelation. An uneasy reverence had set in. There was no more hurried bounding up and down the stairs, with the stairs wildly resounding to everyone's footsteps. Now, it was a purposeful step by step up and down ritual, yet with the still inevitable sounds of the old wood rubbing against old wood. The light in the stairway remained off to allow for a dimly lit tunnel like approach. In a strange way it was like the inner stairway or passageway of the ancient pyramid at Chichen Itza – until someone reached the top of the stairs. In the ancient pyramid a life size carving of a jaguar stood in front of anyone making the inner journey while, here, they entered a room with worn out comfortable furniture and a decorated alter at the window.

Within a day after Shiva's leaving Jane had started working on a collage depicting Shiva's legacy, a collage as symbolic as a Tibetan scroll. Each kept and found memento had been glued or tacked on a large circular wooden board found in the driveway of the hotel. She spray painted a lavender color, largely because that was the only can of spray paint Val had left over. The inner circle was a round mirror with shard of glass glued to it, several with dried up blood on them. Around that circle were larger objects and images – the strangely coded flyer announcing the new disposition, Shiva's epistles, written in a calligraphic flourish, were placed around the flyer and several objects from the beach – a blunt burnt stick with rings of growth showing, oddly enough, the vague markings of the peace symbol. This had become the stick of choice for many scar-desiring followers. The words of his song: *Beautiful Hands* was another item on the outer circle.

She had also hung beads on the doorway of the room while setting up a table in front of the window with a batik cloth covering it in such a way that an image of a single lotus could be seen hanging in front of the table. On this cloth she had placed a single candle within a bowl of sand from the beach. Surrounding this were sticks of incense embedded in the sand with the aroma of sandalwood permeating the room. Others had left small gifts or votive offerings on the newly consecrated alter – shells, a small statue of a Buddha, a note card, a piece of driftwood with a charred end…A hallowed place had grown out of Shiva's mysterious departure.

Marshall had rented the room across the hall and he had become the unofficial guardian of the shrine. He could usually hear someone come up the stairs and if there were no squeaks he could hear the beads rattling if someone entered.

36

Lifeguard

Schilling had not intended to visit the Grandiose as a supplicant or pilgrim but more as a lifeguard to save his friend who had gone under the spell of, what he thought, was an ideological demigod. He considered this a last ditch rescue effort with the intention of slapping Damian back into sensibility. He walked up the driveway of the Grandiose and turned right, opened the weathered screen door that led into the old porch. From there he could see a number of people in the kitchen, several were surrounding Jane, or Starburst, as she now wanted to be called, who was excited and animated, giving directions to several young people Schilling had seen gathered around Shiva the day he had talked to him in his tiki torch throne on the beach. Sweet was one of them.

Yes, I was one of them that day, in the kitchen with Starburst and Surfer and Damian and geez I don't remember who else but Starburst was organizing this memorial to Helen and we all thought it would be a great idea. It was going to be the first gathering of the *Traveling Troupe of Ecstatic Players*, I think that's what we finally called ourselves, Surfer had written a song for the girl, this fallen angel, as we came to call her, and he was going to let me play the tambourine, I needed something, I wanted to get out of this mood that I had been in ever since Surfer and I came back from the beach that day, we were on such a high that I can't tell you what a conflict of emotions I felt. It was like meeting a Greek chorus at the fire station, all talking at once about the crazy departure of Shiva, I couldn't believe it, I didn't know what to think. It took me days to get myself going again. It was like I had lost a reason for going on. Shiva had become my reason, our reason, a vortex around which we revolved – his mysterious disappearance or I would now say his *mysterium*, the event that took on mystical proportions, left us with a huge loss but also with questions as to how to continue. When we heard about the girl who had been shot on Wharf Road it was like the sky fell in, the clouds grew darker and overtook a lot of us. Thank god I had Surfer at the time. He just wasn't going to let all this affect him. We were in love and that is what got us through. We were going to create something positive out of the ashes of that fiery bird, out of the pain that we felt, that is why this memorial was such a good idea. Sunburst came up with something that let us put all our doubts and pain into some transcending energy. We weren't sure what or who would contribute, remember, it was our first gathering. We knew Surfer had a song and I was going to play the tambourine and Starburst was going to invoke the spirit of healing with her bowls and bells…

Schilling's eyes fell on Damian who was sitting at the table engrossed in conversation. "Damian," he called out, putting a brake on the whole scene. "I've got to talk to you!" For a moment he had all eyes on him. They could feel the intensity of his mutton-chopped face and gave him room. Damian looked up, surprised to see his old friend after all the strange and tragic events that had occurred and especially after their falling out.

"Schilling," he quietly responded, "what are you doing here?"

Someone gave him a seat and they faced each other for the first time since their meeting on the beach. Schilling sat down, his body tense, enervated, much like Damian remembered when he would listen to him entertain with stories fished out of the everyday and embellished into dramatic states and, on occasion, laugh that outrageous full- bellied laugh when he made a particularly glib observation.

"Damian," he said again, "I'm leaving." That was it. He left room for a response but Damian did not answer right away…"We can both go back to Michigan if you can let go of this cult stuff?"

With that statement, loud enough for everyone to hear, a change of incredibility came over the room. The silence weighed them down until Damian finally answered in a calm and settled, almost sad, voice, "Albert, I think you still don't understand. My life has changed. Just because Shiva is gone doesn't mean my life hasn't changed. No amount of running is going to bring me back to what I was. I know there will be loss…I would like to have you travel with me my old friend, we've been through a lot…"

168

"What about your wife and your kids? Are you just...?"

"Albert," Damian stopped him, "I am not through with them. They are in the world like I am. Some time, I am hoping, in the future, I am hoping, they will understand that lives change, sometimes radically. I couldn't take the kids away from Cindy. I won't be with them on a day to day basis but I will always be in their lives..."

"How?"

"Sounds like Hollywood...sorry, I didn't mean to make light of this but it's not like you haven't had some traumatic changes in your life. We were friends when you crashed and burned. Remember? You spent hours on that pillow chanting yourself into some other world or trying to forget the one you left..."

"Yes, but I did not leave two kids..."

"Do you think for one minute you wouldn't have – you had left everything that you loved? Am I right or what?"

"Damian." This time the voice was like aloe vera smoothing over the pain felt by the two old friends, "We're heading out. Jane wants us to help up set up the bowls. Can we..."

The softness of her words put a halt to their verbal sparring or argument or discussion, like a breeze she touched them both. Schilling's idea of bringing sense back into Damian evaporated with that voice. Damian turned his head and just smiled, "Remember Tanya," he said to Schilling, "my awakening..."

Schilling could only acknowledge her. There was something about her that intrigued him. Damian was right about her dark eyes, which were surrounded by short curly black hair and her pert full lips. He said he fell into her mouth, well that may or may not be an exaggeration, I can see that but you don't leave everything just for a trip into the sensual world, or do you?

"Albert," Damian finally said, "I've even written some words for this lovely lady – it's called Dark-eyed Jewel. Here's a short taste of it, *dark-eyed jewel*

Black as all the colors giving up their light
When you're near
There's something in the air that's going to come out right
I feel it here
A rainbow's coming...

With these words he looked up at Tanya only to see her gesturing..."Hey, I'm needed. Listen, Albert, please, pick up your harmonica, I've been trying to talk to Cindy, she's obviously upset, if you see her when you get back, relay a message to her and the kids, will you. They will always be in my life. I can only hope that someday the kids will understand, sometimes a person must take a different path, whether he's a father or not. Tell them my love will still be with them..."

With that wishful pronouncement he and Tanya moved into the bustle of people carrying blankets, bowls, batiks and food and heading out the back door, leaving Schilling to contemplate the inevitable, that this would be his last day in Bolinas. It was time to pack up and say goodbye to the bikers at Smileys, he thought, and...maybe if he has time, pay his respects to the 'fallen angel'.

The house was quiet when he finally got up. With a slow thoughtful sighing, he seemed ready to leave but something wouldn't let him just go out the backdoor. Out of curiosity he turned towards the stairs and walked through the opening, into the long dimly lit upward passageway, up slowly up, there was no Marshall in the adjacent room, all was quiet, up slowly up, until he parted the beads and saw the table under the window. No candle was glowing but the afternoon sun had just begun to send light through the upper window. He stood there wondering, waiting until a shaft of light struck the figure of the Buddha. He smiled. Wouldn't you know it, he thought, even the sun has to tempt my doubter's mind; every day it comes through here, following a preordained path and sinking into the west, every day it shines some rays of light through this window and everyday it illuminates something and it just so happens that this time it illuminated a Buddha figure, a full bodied, Buddha-bellied, laughing Buddha figure - illuminating this moment, illuminating this symbolic statue of human endearment...of wisdom. What did he see here, in this window, this Shiva character? Did he have the same light coming through that I'm seeing? Did his imagination just go wild?

In the stillness, however, even Schilling felt an otherworldlyness, which he would later call a *contemplative pause*. We can be busy doinggoinglooking, he thought, you name it, and sometimes when we stop in the silence, when we listen in the silence, sometimes, if we are not afraid, sometimes we may hear something else...

After a long while, the man who had once been entranced by Carlos Castaneda and then thrown him into the questionable bin was now taking up or taking out of that bin something else – was there something to this Shiva character, something to his emphasis on ecstasy – a moment that transcends all others? He would let him go with a question for now, he had to keep some objectivity, he would let the question live with him... with that in mind he turned around and walked down a brighter passageway until the kitchen returned and the street welcomed him...

37

Stanford's Escape

Stanford, too, had cooperated with the Sheriff's office and told his story. This time he was not as anxious to accuse Hollywood, in fact, he suggested to them that the coast guard should be notified as a result of Hollywood's find on the beach. If the scarf had washed up on the beach it was the first real clue of her whereabouts. As a result he had spent practically every day since Helen's death, before he had to get back to the university, driving around the lagoon, along the coast, north and south, clambering up and down the cliffs, looking through his binoculars for any shadowed wave swept rock that might hide a body. He had driven as far north as the coast guard station relaying his information of a missing woman, letting them make copies of Julia's photo as he had done at the sheriff's office. At the end of every day's search, depending on where he ended up he had a long dinner with enough wine to ease his wandering mind and himself before going back to Smileys alone *without a direction known...like a rolling stone...*the first time he heard that song by Dylan he felt some inner connection or, in fact, he pulled over to the shoulder and pulled something out of the song that gave him a voice, an outlet, a way of going outside of his all-consuming obsession. Each time he heard it on a local rock station he remembered a few more words and lines until he just sang it over and over while rounding the curves of Highway One, past Dogtown, through the golden hills to his right and the pastures to his left. When he stopped at the Farm House in Olema he was sung out, his mouth dry, ready for a beer and their famous barbequed oysters. Sitting on the back porch, watching the sun slowly but inevitably fall behind the Point Reyes hills, the evening sky invoked a different sound in him, this time, a symphonic melody, one of his favorites, the haunting melody of the second movement of Beethoven's sixth symphony, it was the sound of deep reds moving into vermilion and golden yellows, until the color of slate defined the shadowed contours of the scattered cloud formations. He wanted, for a few short hours, to lose himself in sound, in sky, in gluttony – another side of oysters, please - this time with a garlic butter sauce, a bowl of the best clam chowder, finished off with cheesecake topped with local blackberries *how does it feel to be on your own no direction known like a complete unknown like a rolling stone*, back, back south, back to the cliffs, just south of Stinson Beach, the nude beach, just over the rocky outcrop separated from the public beach, without any luck, without any signs, it was rocky there and difficult to see…The day waned and this time the evenings repast was prepared at the Sand Dollar where he had local salmon broiled with new potatoes and an appetizer of halved artichokes filled with garlic olive oil and finished off with an Irish coffee. He sat back, his head resting on the lattice work of the patio – somehow, he thought, somehow, he sighed, out of a tired and burdened heart, sitting there, time slowed, somehow he just sat there and decided to let go, she would have to find herself, pull herself out of the seaweed, be found by some other beachcomber, he let go…the Sand Dollar didn't change, the same ocean breeze was moving through, he let go and he changed, got in his car and drove to Bolinas to give them notice of his leaving.

38

Jukebox Therapy

Mariah had not been seen since the day of Helen's untimely death. There was no soup pot in the kitchen sending out enticing aromas of garlic and ginger and the closed sign had remained on her front door. The door had stayed locked. She had slept and listened to her juke box even with the intermittent skips and clicks...and when a particularly appropriate lyric played over and over she just let it she just let it she just let it go for minutes that turned into hours, she allowed an inevitable scratch in the 45s become her mantra, her drone of existence. For days now Josh had knocked on her door as well as every hungry hippie who had become used to her hot cups of soup from the bottomless pot...Who would have guessed that Mariah's reaction to the senseless unpremeditated fear-invoked killing of the young woman in the blossoming of her life, would drive her to become a recluse. Who would have imagined that her best intentions for righting a potential wrong would have gone so wrong? Was she to blame? Or, more appropriately

173

how much was she to blame for this uncalled for tragedy.

The days went by, time had softened her pain and no one had blamed her. Many hands had rapped on her door with no response from her. For anyone waiting and listening, the only response that could be heard through the front door was the repeated lyric from some oldie on her jukebox. Stanford had made it a ritual to stop at her place before he finally settled down in his room at Smileys. It was usually late enough, dark enough and cool enough for him to be the only one listening to the words coming from inside. He had noticed a change in the words from the day she had voluntarily holed herself up in the café. The first time he listened the jukebox was stuck on *do not forsake me on my do not forsake me oh my do not forsake me oh my*, a few nights later be heard *I walk the floor the whole night I walk the floor the whole night I walk the floor the whole night* until the day of his return from the Sand Dollar when he heard *let it be let it be let it be let it be let it be* maybe, he thought, she had turned a corner maybe he had also maybe, maybe it was possible *maybe baby* was it possible? It was possible, wasn't it? Tragedy can recede into the past let it be a new life can begin let it be days of remorse can be overcome let it be even years let it be let it be I can keep wallowing in Julia's memory or I can open up to the future with her as part of my life - a blessing – now that's a word I haven't used for a long time – a blessing that was bestowed on me. She enriched my life and now I can open up to future possibilities, even future relationships, loves, lovers…

The door opened. Mariah stood there in all her earthy beauty, the remains of tears in her face…"

So, what are you doing here?" she said with a questioning smile. He was taken aback. He hadn't expected her to actually be here. He was just listening...

"I, I, I've been listening to the clicks, I mean, the records, I mean the repeated, the stuck records…"

"Yea, that jukebox is a healer, an analyst, eventually it says the right things."

He caught himself and slipped back into a variation of familiar academic jargon, "You may have found a popular version of a feed back loop, a cybernetic top ten."

"Well, it took me through the last week, changed me, or at least, I've changed, look, why don't you come in, I've got some coffee on…"

"Thanks, it's a little late for coffee but…"

"Good lord, that's rich, I've lost track of time here, daysnightsdays who knows I've been closeted off for a while."

"No soup line since that young girl died…"

He let it slip out and immediately felt a twinge. She just sighed and opened the door to let him enter. As his eyes adjusted to the candlelit room he took a few steps in and they settled into two odd chairs around a table decoupaged over 45 rpm record covers, a visual reminder of that jukebox analyst. They let a stillness pervade them, the Beatles had gone home, and eventually Mariah asked him if he had come to grips with the loss of his wife. He swallowed and thought for a moment and finally said, "Every time I thought I had a 'grip', as you say, on her loss, I've let go again. I've made a damn mess of it, if I hadn't pushed it…" his voice started to waver.

"Hey come on…"

"I'm the one who pushed the issue with Hollywood, " he finally blurted out.

"Hey, you can't blame yourself, no one could have predicted…"

I accused him!"

"And I brought the situation to a head, all those kids…they just needed a cause…"

"Who knew that Roderick, this so-called professional weed smoking trigger happy professional…" He left the thought dangling, " Who knew?" he said again as a look of inner remembrance came over him. "That odd woman dressed in seaweed, she told me I would find 'hope and vengeance'…little did I know…"

"Anyone can predict tragedy," Mariah countered, "everybody's story has some pain in it?"

As they talked, the weight of the last few days and weeks seemed to ease.

"You know," Mariah finally said, "There was a flyer under my door about a memorial. Maybe, we, actually I'll speak for myself; maybe I should make that the changing point. I'll open up the kitchen again. There'll be some hungry kids…"

Stanford looked at her, stood up, smiled, "Maybe I'll see you there," he told her as he held out his arms to embrace her. They stood for a long while letting their pain flow down, down, to the very floor boards they stood on…

39

Tintintingling

The tintintingling of finger cymbals could be heard but not yet seen until maroon-robed dancers turned the corner of Wharf Road. Hare Krishna hare Krishna Krishna Krishna hare hare was chanted in time to the cymbalic rhythms. The flowered flowing clothes of at least a hundred young people followed behind swaying, dancing, billowing in the afternoon uplift of cool air from the swollen lagoon. A smaller troupe of concerted and dedicated people from the Grandiose had already wound their way down the road. Many of the curious were following them and joining them. They had also been fortified by the freely ladled black bean soup, with that something special in it. Mariah had been busy making up for lost time. When the cymbal bearers chanted their way past Smileys, Bear, Sidekick and Gene came out with several other denizens of the afternoon saloon.

"There's never a dull moment in this place, " Bear said to no one in particular.

"What the hell is going on now?" Sidekick questioned.

"I think it has to do with the girl that was killed." As he said this he pointed to an enigmatic poster on the telephone pole next to Smileys. In the poster a girl's picture was surrounded by flowers becoming negative and positive and negative again the longer they stared at it, until the flowers eventually allowed the negative spaces to form the words of the impending memorial at the end of Wharf Road.

As they were staring, Schilling came into their focus. He had finally found his way back to Smileys when he noticed Bear and friends. Bear was the first to speak, "What do you say Schilling, is this another one of those happenings?"

Still caught in the reverie of his experience, at the alter of the Grandiose, he was momentarily startled by the gruff voice in the street. He was used to it inside the bar, along with other wild chatter, but here, even with lingering cymbals and chanting, Bear's voice carried weight...

"Mister Bear, "Schilling finally responded, "My notebooks are full of strange and exotic observations."

"I suppose that includes us?" Bear asked facetiously.

"I'll bet he has a whole notebook on Smileys," Sidekick added.

"Well, gentleman, you are definitely a part of this wild, unrehearsed cultural smorgasbord."

"Is that good or what?" Sidekick added.

"I think he means that we've added to his research paper, but things haven't ended yet Schilling, why don't we take a walk on the hippie side, down Wharf Road."

"I think we should take a gander at that..."

"What do geese have to do with this?"

"Jesus, Sidekick, settle down, lets all pay our respects."

After that pronouncement, Schilling and Bear led the leather-clad bikers and habitués of Smileys into the dancing chanting throng...

40

Memorial

Wharf Road was awash with colors moving, billowing, sailing over uneven pavement. No cars couldwould maneuver around the cliff today, only living flowing beings spread their wings between the sandstone walls and the stilt houses and the constantly changing glistening incoming waves of the lagoon. Talk, joints, guitars, cymbals, songs, chants were all swept up in this tidal movement of searching souls – some not even knowing the *what for* of the event, some not caring about anything but the happening of the event, some having deciphered the cryptic poster, some having heard the word going round, some just grooving, some feelin the once upon a time loss that was still present that was is still an open wound to too many people who knew her, who loved her, who would like to move through the pain of their loss, who would love to remember without the pain of their loss, who would love... who wouldcould love like Shiva's inspired love...Shiva had told them in different ways that life had to do with life; that we should try to celebrate the few short years we have   on this planet attempting to live to the fullest; that we should attempt to experience ecstasy on a daily basis by living in the now of ecstatic experience, ecstatic life…

Jane had set up her ceremonial batik blanket on a smooth section of pavement in front of the wall near Helen's tragic resting place on which someone had painted, *here lies a fallen angel*. An outline of her body had also been painted on the pavement. Inside it, people had been throwing flower petals, layers of dying dried out petals were mixed and covered with freshly plucked carminevermillion rose petals, pinkredviolet bougainvillea, whole white daisies with deep brown centers…Jane set her bowls and pillow on the blanket. Surfer had brought his guitar, Sweet, the tambourine, Marshall had carried a long Tibetan horn to the gathering, Hare Krishna could still be heard wafting over them with the tintintingling of finger cymbals accentuating the air…there was a mixture of sadness and exuberance and all manner of moods in between…

When, finally, the sun was in the constellation of Aquarius, when the time seemed right, Marshall took up the horn, took a deep breath, as if to concentrate the atman itself, and blew into the long brass pipe until the air was enervated and vibrating, coming out in low trembling tones, vibrating, undulating over the street, into the living sentient beings, up the cliffside, over the lagoon until the mood began to change, he took another breath and blew again, three times he blew, filling the air with sounds that could pattern swords into symbols of peace, allowing the vibrating pattern enter everyone and everyplace…

When a relative quiet had ensued Jane rubbed her moist finger on a brass bowl setting off a high continuous tone, then another with a different frequency, then another, mixing these cosmic sounds with the ping of brass disks meeting in midair…the mood had become responsive, like the first violin tuning the instruments of a cacophonous orchestra…she hit the bowls softly with a mallet, letting the vibrations reverberate off the bodies and minds of those mingled under the cliff of the mesa and the continuous changing of the sea water. Surfer picked up his acoustic guitar and when the vibrations had settled, let his words flow over the crowd…"this is for a fallen angel who died too soon…"

With a rhythmic beat he sang,

They say the dream has died, they say it's over
They see the turning tide and say it's over
Time it was, time it was
When flowers could be found in the hands of children
Time it was time it was
When flowers could be found in the hands of children

Sweet joined him with the tambourine and they played the tune while Surfer continued,

Sometimes I feel the pain, the pain of knowing
What once was all so clear has clouded over
Time is so time is so
When flowers turn to death in the hands of hatred
Time is so, time is so
When flowers turn to death in the hands of hatred

180

This time a siren screamed into the crowd, a contribution from Marshall who had procured a reasonable facsimile from Val's store.

After several cacophonous instrumental additions, which invoked the tragic street scene, Surfer continued,

They say the dream has died, they say it's over
But I know that dreams can hide until the dawn comes
And the time it is, time it is
When love can be again
And flowers can be found in the hands of children
Time it is, time it is
When flowers can be found in the hands of children
Time it is, time it is
When flowers can be found in the hands of children
Time it is, time it is...

The guitar rhythm continued and the words were repeated until they emptied into the evenings fading light...a few candles could be seen beginning to create shadows around the flowered memory of Helen.

Marshall blew on the horn three times, signaling a change in the flow of the memorial, allowing for response and spontaneity...Hollywood entered the road way, meandering his way through and around seated beings, standing beings, holding his smoldering sage in the air, letting the smoke cleanse and heal just as he had the day of her death...Marshall sat down, cross-legged, near Jane, near Surfer and Sweet, Eden joined them...letting the silence enter, letting the ocean enter, letting the squawk of the seagulls enter..."Let us remember a young girl's life..." Marshall announced in a solemn voice, "let us unite in remembering a young girl's life..." With those words Eden formed his mouth and out of his deep inner breathing self began to sound out...ooommmmmmm ooommmmmmm until others joined him in that vibrating uralt sound of beginnings and endings ooommmmmmmmm Jane circled the bowls with her fingers adding the cosmic connection ooommmmmmmmm the sounds grew until there was a change in the air going out, permeating out into the surrounding hills and the western horizon, listening hearing remembering a young girl's life...

41

Om

Not everyone, however, had pursed their lips and let out the sound of *om*, in fact, at some point, Schilling had begun to drift into his own thoughts. He even remembered Bucky Fuller singing a variation of an old standard – *dome, dome on the range* – which made him think of *om, om at the memorial*, which made him smile a slight guilt-ridden smile. He looked around wondering if anyone else had separated from the overwhelming collective vibration of om. He looked at Bear and Sidekick at the periphery of the crowd. They looked somewhat astonished but their mouths were closed. What were they thinking, he wondered? Stanford was with them. Even he had ventured to take in the reminder of that day. Was he looking for some mental closure to his part in the tragedy?

He continued to scan the crowd, most of the faces were contorted into the sound of om...except that Hollywood was still smudging the air, circling the flower-petaled reminder of Helen, stepping around the seated flower children and helping to let the thoughts of her short lived life come into them. Schilling continued searching the faces, wondering, until he saw Mariah's face. She was standing in the midst of several young girls, one with auburn hair flowing over her shoulders. The girls were standing close to the earth mother, the dispenser of soup and love. Most likely they were friends of Helen's, and here, they had taken refuge in the folds of Mariah's aprons, all surrounded by the vibrations of om...

Schilling's eyes remained on her until, until she also strayed, for a moment, from her thoughts of Helen and the young friends surrounding her, until her head turned and she smiled, slightly, at the mutton-chopped Schilling, a smile of shared life experience. They connected until she turned her head to meet the gaze of the man she had held the night before, when the repeated sound of let it be let them be in their emotional commiseration of loss, unknown loss and known loss, loss so hard to let go and yet, as her gaze met his eyes and connected over the sound of om, there was an overtone of inner emotional vibration. Somehow it satisfied both of them, warmed them, their momentary connection allowed the om to pass, the sound of three blasts of the Tibetan horn to pass, the tintintingling of the hare Krishna's to pass, the slow letting go of all those flowing blowing mind bending sending thoughts of healing to pass...until Wharf Road had enough room for Stanford and Mariah and even Schilling to merge in recognition and physical closeness, a rendezvous they had not necessarily anticipated. Stanford would later think of it as going back to the mother, for warmth and security. Schilling would later see it as the beginning of a simpatico relationship. She put her arms in both of their arms. They both smiled a kind of understanding smile, as they all wound their way back to Scowleys, talking of endeavors to come, of future callings and plans to be made and plans to be. Stanford, of course, was heading back to the university and let her know how timely her jukebox therapy had been, or was it her black bean soup for the soul, that had warmed him. Schilling, of course, was returning to Detroit, to put some literate coherence on these last few weeks. And she, she was going to continue running Scowleys, dispensing soup and keeping the café going, getting Hollywood to do some fixing up, but her plans did not preclude the possibility of visiting either Stanford at the university or visiting Schilling, that is, if she could take time off from her one-woman café and save the money for airfare. Schilling offered to help and she was receptive.

It turned out that the opportunity came the following summer after Schilling had gone into summer break from teaching introductory humanities classes at the Community College. He helped pay the airfare and she ended up in the Detroit airport waiting for him to pick her up. They had much to talk about on the way to his small over crowded apartment across from the Fisher Theater and around the corner from Woodward Avenue. Their long awaited rendezvous in the motor city had all kinds of possibilities. He was going to take her to the Institute of Art to show her the new Caravaggio that was just purchased for close to a million dollars, but mainly he was going to take her to the medieval courtyard, in the interior of the Art Institute building, that had been turned into a café. It had become the gathering place of any number of poets, artists, and teachers from Wayne State University, hangers-on, and visitors to the museum. He told her about the *turkeys* who gathered there on Sunday mornings reading the New York Times, momentarily wandering into the current events of the world and any other tangents their creative minds could add to the news. Conversation usually turned into what the afternoon's sojourn might have to offer – sometimes a tour of a new exhibit – definitely the Caravaggio – or a deepening of the on-going exhibits, sometimes a trip to Belle Isle to float down the Detroit River on rented canoes...He laughed his full-bellied laugh as he described the *turkeys* - Freddie the fox, Phil the paver, El Lobo, Zee – until they drove closer to Woodward Avenue and saw smoke billowing in the air, until they heard the sirens, until they saw crowds in the street ahead of them, crowds of largely, African American youths running away from tear gas and the police...They were almost caught up in the riots that would engulf portions of the city...but that is another story. They were able to drive out of the danger, the frustrations, the pent up anger of a thousand young people caught up in destroying, for many reasons, caught up in destroying...

They drove to his brother's home in the suburbs of Detroit, a safe haven for now, where they could watch the burning of the city in the comfort of his living room...Schilling's neighborhood was on TV...It would not be the same, in the aftermath, it would not be the same and they, they would continue to see each other over the years, remembering, remembering...

42

Marshall's Journey

After Jane's spiritually transcending ritual in the midst of many responsive souls, after the VW van had been packed with bells and bowls and cushions and teas and enough snacks from the General Store to feed her and Surfer and Sweet and Eden and several other eager disciples, after they bowed to the Princess, the Pacific, the Mesa and finally to Bolinas, after Surfer blew on the conch and all had climbed on board, after the actual van had ceased to exist for Marshall looking out the west facing window of revelation, there was a profound yet strange mixture of feelings welling up in him. He did not want them to leave without him yet he did not want to leave...he wanted them around him, yet he did not want to leave, his encounters with Shiva had changed him, at least he thought they had changed him, his encounters with Jane and their philosophical schism had both frustrated and enervated him – he felt alive in these emotional outbursts and resulting whirlpools. Standing there, looking at what might have been, he thought of Eden and those who had stayed with him, Damian, Tanya, they had not left, as well as the numerous followers who had come to Bolinas; those who had heard about Shiva, heard his message, who were curious…

Marshall was determined to stay in the opposite room of the Grandiose, watching, guarding, leading the curious to the message and the memory of the 'master' who had ascended. He wanted to keep his encounters and his moments with the 'master' alive. It was not the free flowing cannabis or other mind bending drugs that had affected him but the deep visceral emotional intense experiences that had occurred once twice several times in his dervish dance with Shiva. In those moments he felt the way he always thought he should feel or should have felt in the world, in his relationship with his mother, his father – to bring it all back home he thought of John Lennon's song, *momma don't go oooo daddy come hooooome momma don't gooooooooo daddy come hooooooome…*That screaming desperation was as close as a song could get to his own cry in the wilderness of need *momma don't gooooooo oo daddy come hooooo ommmm…*

But the wild ness would not let him go no matter how hard he tried to settle in. He needed confrontation and Shiva had gone and Jane was on her way to enlighten the world. To be a guide, or a disciple was not his forte. Even being the guardian of the shrine was not satisfying him. When a month had passed he decided to go back to San Francisco moving into the Baker Hotel off Polk Strasse. There was action there, the street was alive with hustlers, leather clad with butts showing, literally two half moons surrounded by black leather chaps. It was a time of liberation and personal rights individual rights gay rights and somehow this became his rallying cry. Somehow he had always suspected his attempted relationships with women were forced, it was more like serious play to see who could end up on top – it was a battle of wits, particularly with a certain woman he met at the Network Coffeehouse. She sat there, on a high perch, at a round table, almost every night. She controlled her space and fondled her Tarot cards, telling fortunes, if someone was willing and ready to listen. He had his future laid out several times only to see the grim reaper come up once to often. It made him reject the cards and her credibility but he continued to see her. He liked her banter and stayed in her presence until she was ready to go home, she had a legitimate job in the morning. Nine o'clock was her midnight, but nine was just his beginning. This was the time he ventured into the peep show parlors, one, in particular, that he had gotten to know. There was no restraint in those heady, lustful, *anything goes* days. He had found his place in his own booth just like the Tarot woman at the coffee house. He had found his place putting quarters into the slot choosing from a variety of x-rated super 8 films or, on occasion, going to see the live girls in another parlor. From the confines of a booth he could watch them dance and if he shoved enough dollars through a slit under the window, he could have them dance next to his window, rubbing their pubic hair on the glass. But, more and more, he watched the films, which allowed his voyeuristic tendencies to grow. At first it was the heterosexual sex that he couldn't get enough of. He liked the spouting of whale-sized men on to the faces of open-mouthed women, but it seemed he was only satisfied for a while. He was always looking for more and more bizarre depictions – all the variations of sexual encounters, no holes barred, he couldn't get enough, he couldn't satiate himself, it got to the point where relieving himself was not enough, he ended up going into a booth that had a three inch hole bored into the side at a convenient height. Now he could lure an equally desperate man with his bait, hoping for some response but it was the sight of other softhard members poking through that really turned him on, now he could put his lips on that member and suck until he heard the anonymous guy in the next booth moan, until he shot the hot mixture of a million lost sperm into his mouth - from no one he knew, only the hardened member of the male species wantingneeding to feel the physical orgasm of ecstasy…again…again…and again… It became a routine for him until he saw the death card, only this time it was the grim reaper appearing over his bed in his closet room. He continued to listen to Handel, he continued to go to the opera, he saw the Duncan Dancers, but he always came back to the x rated peepshow parlor in a spiral of flooding cum until Eden saw him one day, hobbling up Sutter Street to go to a bookstore he worked at part time. He had gotten fleshy, limping, looking like he was in pain. He caught up with him, only to see his intensity gone. The vital searching human being he remembered was now a pained, fat, clown like personage, hardly recognizable…

"Marshall, Marshall, how are you?"

Marshall looked, his eyes opened wider, only a slight smile of acknowledgement came from him.

Eden did not push anything. He let Marshall decide the pace. After a while, Marshall looked over to Eden and said in a matter of fact voice, "Eden, I have aids…"

There was no response from Eden. They walked silently together past a gay bar that had music blaring into the street, *momma don't go ooooooooooo, daddy come hoooooooommmmmmmm momma don't gooooooooo oooooo daddy come hoooooo oooommmmmmmmmmm*…That song stayed with him until the end, until he settled his affairs, willing whatever money he had saved into paying for the west-facing room at the Grandiose Hotel, until his money ran out, or until someone else continued to venerate the window of revelation and the candlelit shrine to an enlightened master…the master who had flown…

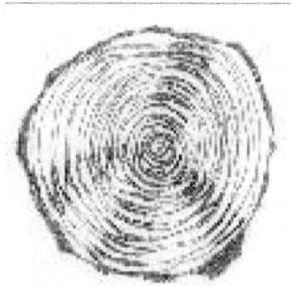

43

Caravansary

No matter how exalted the desire to make an offering to the world the attempt is still rooted in tomorrow's practical and physical reality. This was soon apparent as Jane's caravan of ecstatic players wound its way north along the coast, along that fabled highway. Just outside of Fort Bragg the transmission gave out on the VW van. They pooled their meager savings and had the van towed to a local garage. While waiting for a newused transmission, Jane, forever the optimist, forever seeing an opportunity in adversity, set up her ceremonial bowls and bells in the nearby park. Tree lined and shady, she chose a sun-washed grassy opening amidst the long established oaks to send out the vibes. When all was set, Surfer blew the Tibetan horn to wake up the locals from their somnambulistic state and proceeded to try and transform, not only the park, but also, the town. Just by being there, Jane and troupe created conversation and response – some simply ignored them, others shook their heads and passed by, eventually the local cop drove up, watched and listened and drove on, no harm done...*nothing to get hung up about...strawberry fields forever*...Some passing people did stop, however, and sat down on the dilapidated benches ringing the interior of the park, or just plopped themselves on the dandelion blooming grass, wondering about this uninvited invasion of their sleepy public place, their peace...

After the barrage of the ten-foot long Tibetan horn, Jane tuned the air with her finger bowl inducing ethereal sounds, while Sweet proceeded to make a garland of the golden dandelions. A suited dude from the modest city hall ventured to ask what the occasion was?

Sweet, who was closest to him answered, "We are sending out the vibes of an ascended master."

"Sounds a bit *far out* as some would say."

"He was in Bolinas and touched a lot of us."

"Now it sounds a bit racy."

"Not in an obscene way, he touched us in a beautiful way, we felt him physically and spiritually..."

"So, what are you sending out?"

Surfer, who was listening, added his own understanding of their newly instigated mission to the world, "Well, we aren't selling anything, we're just relating what happened to us in the presence of Shiva."

"Shiva?"

"That's what he was known to us when we first met him, but he became a master or guru for a lot of us and we want to spread his thoughts on living here...now..."

"So, like what kind of thoughts?"

"Well, let me pose them the way he did with us. Are you living to your full capacity?"

He shrugged, not sure what to say.

"Well, have you had an orgasm lately?"

Taken back, he just slightly smiled.

"That's what he was about. He tried to have us live more intensely, by trying to break through our routine reality, he wanted us to live more like we were having an orgasm every day, every hour, every minute..."

"Jesus, I'd probably die."

When she heard that, Jane smiled and said, "You might."

"But no one can live like that."

"But we can get closer to it..."

"This is getting a little weird for me, Thanks, I have to be back. This was lunch for me."

At this point Surfer picked up his guitar, started a reggae rhythm, to be joined by Sweet on the tambourine and started quietly singing a new song he had been working on, a round for the earth that, hopefully, would be catchy enough to set the place in motion and have others join in. Just barely audible, he started the round,

Don't forget the earth sustains you
Just don't let the pavement take you
From the source of life around you
Don't forget the earth sustains you

Don't forget the earth becomes you
Just don't let the fools take from you
All the promise of your birthright
Don't forget the earth becomes you
After a few repeats and building in volume, he sang the verse,
And I'm singing
Yes I'm singing
Ah ah awe
Ah ah awe
Of forest wanderings
Of prairie sunsets
And the beauty of it all
Yes the beauty of it all
At this point Sweet joined him, picking up the words, as the rounds to the earth continued,
And I'm singing
Yes I'm singing
Ah ah awe
Ah ah awe
Of ocean mysteries
Rivers that run free
And the beauty of it all
Yes the beauty of it all
Jane, in a flowing dress and a found jesters hat, began to dance with a combination of Egyptian gestures and Beach Boys surfing movements. An hour or two went by with the troupe trying out different ways of creating an *ecstatic happening*. When the rounds had ended and their energy had dissipated around the park, the common ground, Surfer went to the garage to pick up the van.

From this beginning they traveled further north, stopping in at places they knew, putting on impromptu performances, slowly getting some routines in place, but keeping any performance as spontaneous as possible. By the time they crashed in a commune in Cave Junction, Oregon they had songs, dances, spoken epistles by Shiva, as part of their repertoire as well as the introductory mood setting bowls and bells and, of course, the Tibetan horn of beginning and ending..."

They stayed several weeks at the commune, helping to harvest tomatoes and cucumbers for some great Greek salads with the commune's goat feta cheese. They picked apples and helped clear land for additional fields of plenty. By the time they were ready to travel eastward, they had had evenings of songs and stories, especially of their time in Bolinas and Shiva's incredible new age ministry, short and intense as it was. The story of this unique spiritual master had preceded them to the commune and every bit of information about him was talked about over supper and in the fields. There was talk of sightings but nothing concrete, hearsay that some one looking like him had passed through Eugene or other towns as far north as Cascade but there was no forwarding address, only an increasing aura of mystery. The day they left Cave Junction several commune members joined them in an old pick-up truck that they had painted in rainbow colors – aqua blue to forest green to golden yellow to vermillion to fuchsia. After they had crossed the Tetons and arrived in Jackson Hole, they had added a camper to the pick up and a Volkswagen joined them, driven by a bearded accordion player, who was as eager as Jane in creating street theater, puncturing the status quo and questioning the routine realities of the locals.

As they neared Madison, Wisconsin, the news of their caravan had already brought about an anticipation that allowed them to stay in the university dorms and headline a weekend *be in*, a human *be in*...

By now they had learned their song well and were ready to sing it, they had found their diverse voices and were ready to voice them and it was a joy it was a joy it was an ecstatic joy that swept through the crowd. Alan was there playing his squeeze box singing *tiger tiger burning bright in the middle of the night*...Timothy was there telling everyone to *turn on tune in and drop out*...Shiva was there in the voices of Surfer and Sweet and Jane who were by now speaking and singing in the rhythms of a ritual Mass:

It began with the blowing of the horn of beginning, three times, until the crowd noticed...Jane tuning the air and the surrounding vibes with the brass bowls...in the midst of high pitched vibrations, the cosmic echoes of her bowls, Surfer began a C chord arpeggio on his acoustic guitar, the individual tones played through a pattern of chord changes, Sweet joined him when he began to sing, echoing the words,

The sky is beginning beginning beginning
The fire is still is still is still
The woods are of ages
The river is still is still is still
The sky is beginning beginning beginning
Is there time?
time time for us?
Is there time?
time time enough?
Is there time?
time time for us?

Jane lightly pounded the brass bowls with a soft mallet letting them vibrate at different frequencies, over and over, until the ringing resounded over the grass and into every ear and into every human being listening and hearing and just be ing there...

The sky has no ending no ending no ending
The fire keeps burning keeps burning keeps burning
The woods are a mystery
The river keeps flowing keeps flowing keeps flowing
The sky has no ending no ending no ending
You and I
Walk on a common ground

194

You and I
sing out a needed sound
You and I can turn the earth around
The earth is beginning beginning beginning...bells gongs bowls...the words ended ended ended, the arpeggios died out, the bowls softly screamed for a while longer until Eden blew on the horn three more times... when the cosmic tones had finally spread beyond them, Surfer spoke slowly evoking the voice of Shiva – "We must disregard fears, the fears of the unknown. They can grow inside us. They are inside us just as surely as they seem to come from outside us. In order to live with them we must live as if we had already died. Then each act would be free of fear. This is the faith of the fulfilled human being.
His message to all of us was and is...
To be passionate...
To let ecstasy enter your life...
He repeated,
To let ecstasy enter your life...thus spake Shiva, the enlightened one...at some point an accordion with a touch of zydeco slapped everyone in the face, woke them up, shook them out of their laid back concentration and momentary *reverence*...after enough energy had been spent a reggae rhythm on the guitar let everyone sway and eventually join in on the round,
Don't forget the earth sustains you
Just don't let the pavement take you
From the source of life around
Don't forget the earth sustains you...by this time Sweet was singing the verses,
And I'm singing
Yes I'm singing aw ah awe aw ah awe...that was quite often the routine and the frame work that they played with which allowed for variations and extemporaneous additions...when the time came and things were mellow enough the horn of the ending was again blown three times...
After this new age Mass another band took center stage, starting with a familiar tune eventually moving into drawn out riffs and meandering melodies until the dancing swaying moving flowered children were no longer able to stand until they sat and finally slept for a while on their blankets and sleeping bags. Even then there was no sleep in the usual sense...
During the second day's high jinks and low jinks and happenings and performances and rainbow highs and mellow grooving, Alan said to Tim, "Can you imagine if we are right?"
The *be in* brought many people to Madison, even a contingent from Vermont. They had been fascinated by the traveling troupe of ecstatic players and talked to Jane about coming to Vermont. They had a farm with enough land to bring about another *be in*. In fact, they told her they could stay for the winter and help create a yearly celebration. The plans were already in place for an amphi-theater to be built in a special location

195

on the land. Before the last sleeping bag had been rolled up most of the troupe had decided to go – the movement was gathering momentum...

"Well, now you know how I got to Vermont," Sweet suddenly broke from the mood of the story and brought it home and up to date, "It was a long strange trip...We held things together for a few years but we, I now think, we had chipped away at the foundation of our postwar culture and society so much that we had a hard time finding our own or building our own. We tried to reinvent everything, from basic family relationships to working together. Questioning everything can only last so long before you have to solidify somewhere somehow...And so, that's what happened, I wanted to buy this farm and stay and build and have a family and Surfer missed the ocean, the waves, actually, I think, he didn't know how to settle down. I probably didn't either but I wanted to try. We talked and reminisced and cried and even made love until we finally agreed that we would take a break. The night he left I asked him to let me know what was happening in Bolinas. I think I even asked him if the missing woman had ever been found. He said he would send me all the news. The news I got back, however, was that he had been drafted soon after he went back to California...and sent to Vietnam. I never saw him again. He was my first real love. We found each other on that soft bed of pine needles...

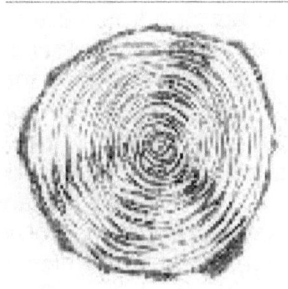

11

Father and Sons

Some years after the summer of ecstasy and tragedy a father with two boys took a turn down a tunneled, tree-lined lane going south, off Highway One. They were exploring the coast. The boys had tuned into a local radio station, heard a driving down beat and *found a way the other day to leave the crowds that are,*
So caught in hot pursuit,
So caught in makin loot,
Such crazy ways
Oh nooooooooo just let yourself goooooooo,
travelin on highway one,
travelin on highway one…
mmmm mmmm travelin on highway one
feelin the touch of the winnnnd
No matter where you've been no matter what you've done you'll feel like you have just begun travelin on highway one
travelin on highway one,
Found a way the other day to leave a state of mind

Brought on by world news
Brought on by narrow views
Oh no ooo just let yourself goooo
Travelin on highway one

Travelin on highway one...They had been through Point Reyes Station and Olema and gone past Dogtown (now with a population of 15) wandering, weaving turning...their open car windows permeated by the pungent oil of eucalyptus. For the sheer joy of discovery, the father drove straight down a tree-lined lane instead of turning left on the designated highway. The road continued straight until the explorers found themselves in the no name town of Bolinas. They parked the car on the Main Street, walked past Smileys and went into the General Store. They paid for drinks and granola bars and asked the clerk, who looked like a generic grandfather, for places to stay. He told them about the Grandiose Hotel right around the corner. That was their introduction to the old two-room hotel. After they had walked past the bricbrac and the antiques and the vintage clothing and the old 45s of the store the father inquired about a room. Val told him the back room was available. At $33 per night the price was considerably below the current bed and breakfast cost of $100 per night and up. In this case there was no breakfast included but there were tea bags on the kitchen table. They signed up, paid for two nights and took their bags through the back door. The washer and dryer were still in the back porch and the bathroom still had a claw foot tub and still needed repainting. The kitchen had the smell and look of years of lived in activity with the soft and round edges on the sink counter and the old table and chairs as well as the bowed floorboards. The unlocked screen door still allowed for the incoming cool breezes from the lagoon to flow through and into the kitchen.

"We're here," the father said, holding his arms out, "Is this funky enough?" There wasn't much response, maybe, even some vague grumbling but his enthusiasm did not wane and he led the way up the stairs, still creaking, to the open door on the left, the right door to the west facing room being closed and presumably locked. They entered and the two boys immediately leaped onto a double bed lodged between the rafters of the attic like room. As they got closer to the window, sunlight bathed them and let them revel in the warmth. The furniture of cast-offs and worn out country antiques looked like a trip to grandmother's house. There was a porcelain basin, with a pitcher inside, standing on the dresser, making the room appear like some thing out of the old west or westerns on TV. Did Bret Maverick stay here and freshen up with eau de cologne, before the customary poker game at the local saloon.

"Hey, listen up, you two, don't destroy the place, we just got here..." His admonition fell on deaf ears until the younger child bounced too high and hit his head on the angled ceiling.

"See I told you, why does it have to get to that point...come here, let's see..."

He examined the wincing head, held his face between his hands, looked at him and smiled. "You're OK, what do think of the place?"

"I like it, Dad."

"See, we don't have to have a hot tub every time we stay over night."

"I do," said the older brother, "but I guess I can handle this for one night."

"Hey, waddya say I read something to you before we roam around the town."

He pulled a dog-eared novel out of his backpack, opened it up to a marked page, told them it was by a guy named Kerouac and started reading,

...and I shambled after as I've been doing all my life after people who interest me, because the only people for me are the mad ones, the ones who are mad to live, mad to talk, mad to be saved, desirous of everything at the same time, the ones who never yawn or say a commonplace thing, but burn, burn, burn like fabulous yellow roman candles exploding like spiders across the stars and in the middle you see the blue centerlight pop and everybody goes "Awww!"

By the time he got to the third page he was in sync with the rhythm of the words, rolling, jumping off the page coming alive...an hour went by and the kids hadn't physically moved but by the looks on their rapt faces they had traveled with him...It was not a story told in the way they were used to – they were brought up on fairy tales, and Norse myths and King Arthur's knights. Stories out of another Western canon and ingrained in their cultural psyches – told through grandmothers and grandfathers, and compiled by story tellers; told through their first readings and plays and teachers...What did this syncopated odyssey have to do with them? It was the way the father read it. One moment they had their foot on the brakes and the next moment they were pushing the gas pedal to the floor until they drove over the whole afternoon, until they finally decided to leave their driver's seats. But before bounding down the stairs, they became aware that the door across the hall was slightly ajar. They stopped, noticed the smell of incense and the flickering light coming through the crack...Their curiosity was piqued but it did not deter them from running out of the house and continuing down Wharf Road to a boat pier where they watched a small motorboat, with fishing poles, tie up.

"Did you catch anything?"

"Take a look..."

A cooler was opened and they could see three silver-speckled glistening salmon, about 20 inches long.

"Wow." Both boys reacted with some amazement.

"Looks like barbeque time," the father said.

"Actually, they're going to the local restaurant."

"That's a good idea for dinner. Waddya say kids?"

"Yea..."

"There's only one problem. The local restaurant tonight is not the Shoppe but a real local home style restaurant."

"What do you mean?"

"Well, look, if you guys can keep a secret, it's called the Monday Night

Eatery."

"And?"

"It's only open Monday nights when the Shoppe is closed."

"Sounds good."

"Except only locals and friends can go to it."

"I guess that leaves us out."

"Well, if I give you the pass word they'll let you in…"

"Now, it's becoming mysterious. We wouldn't mind going though. What do you say kids?"

They shrugged their shoulders, "OK."

"Alright, the password is *spice box* and it's in a house on the Mesa. You take a right past the Post Office and follow the road up until it begins to turn left. It's the house on the right, in the trees. There should be cars parked out front."

"I think you've added a bit of mystery to our tour. Thanks. We'll call it *The Adventure of the Wild Salmon.*"

They said goodbye and continued along the lagoon, past the dentist's office, where they heard a rustle from the overgrown vegetation by the cliff. The father thought it was probably a raccoon and they all walked on. When they got to the boulders marking the entrance to the beach he noticed the remains of an old weathered peace sign on the sea wall of the lagoon. It was a quick glance; the kids were already running on the beach. He looked long enough to make out faded letters above the sign…*a fallen angel who left too soon…*

He just wondered, went on, took a few steps and jumped onto the sand; feeling exhilarated…yet the angel lingered. The after noon sunlight pervaded, warmed them, even in the coolness of the incoming ocean breeze. The kids were taking running starts up the cliff side until they had to turn around and roll back down. There was no over hanging gazebo above them; there was no heavy metal band playing for the seagulls. It was an uneventful Monday afternoon with little activity except for a couple of dogs running free. He sat on a partially buried driftwood log and scanned the view from the western sunset to the east. The hills had turned a lilac red with the contrasting coastal oaks arranging patterns on the light brown grass. This is as it should be, he thought, how fortunate to be here with these two young growing…

"Dad," the youngest cried out, "come on over…"

He smiled.

"How high can you go?"

Well, he couldn't ignore a challenge; after all, he still had something to teach these kids. He took off his backpack, got a running start and headed straight up, touching the cliff at least 5 feet above them, falling backwards, slipping, rolling back down. He lay still…

"Dad, dad, are you OK?"

No response.

They hurried to him…

"Wahhhhhh!" he yelled, jumped up and tackled them. Laughing and rolling down the eroded sand stone hill they finally ended up sprawled on the solid beach. Laughing and holding them was like wanting to stop time, to stop from changing, changing them, changing the moment. He was them, they were him, they were…while the princess of Tamalpais looked on, turning into shades of gray. A belt of yellow hovered over the western horizon and underneath a huge cloud cover.

"Anyone getting hungry?"

"Yea, yea…"

"Shall we try to find this mystery place?"

"OK, we could try," the youngest said, while the oldest gave out a tepid, "I guess."

They took the Brighton Road back to the Grandiose, washed up and decided to walk up the road.

"It gets kind of spooky in these trees…"

"Monster trees…"

"Giant trees waiting to grab young boys…"

Before they went any further a cool wind whipped through the high eucalyptus trees and got the blackberry bushes moving, when the wail of a banshee sounded, the boys were in hysterics…

"Dad, dad, where are you?"

"Ooooooooooeeeeeeeeeeeoooooooooooo…"

"Dad!!!" Come on…"

Something, out of nowhere, out of the darkness, jumped behind them.

"Ooooooooeeeeeeeee…"

They turned in terror, only to make out it was their father flailing his arms as he wailed.

"Dad, dad, dang it now you you…"

Laughing now, he grabbed them…

"Did I scare you?"

"Yea."

"I don't think I want to do this."

"Oh, come on now, you wouldn't let your old Dad scare you, would you?"

"No, but, why are we doing this?"

"Because, because, it's a mystery, remember, and we're detectives on a case, remember, I said this *was the Adventure of the Wild Salmon*, well now we've added, or the wind added, the wail of a long ago death on the Mesa. Maybe she's coming to haunt us…it's one case Dr. Watson didn't write down."

"That's because he never came to California."

"That's right, so keep good notes. We may need a chronicler."

"Who's Dr. Watson?"

"He was Sherlock Holmes' right hand man."

"And he wrote down the adventures, right?"

"Right, so keep your eyes peeled."

As they rounded the hill they did find several cars parked outside of an overgrown fence set among the eucalyptus. Finding a path to a door they knocked.

"Who is it?"

"We were, ahh, wondering about…is the restaurant open?"

"I don't know."

"It's called *spice box* isn't it?"

"You got that right."

The door opened and a graying slightly balding man let them in. Laughter and talking greeted them. Several couples were seated at a variety of small tables and there were seats at a picnic size table in the, what looked like a, dining room. Their eyes widened to the party atmosphere and especially to the rooms stuffed with antiques and artifacts and found objects – shells, driftwood, dolls made from twigs…

Everywhere you looked there were mementos of years of living in the house. It had turned into a living museum along with the requisite cobwebs. They sat down and nodded hello to a couple already sitting at the table, while their host told them to go into the kitchen for the specials of the evening.

"Fresh salmon today, poached or broiled, and our regular linguini with our own meat sauce."

They eased into the narrow kitchen. The kids helped themselves to linguini while he chose the broiled salmon. There was salad and plenty of garlic bread to go along with the entree. When they were seated again, the father asked the couple at the table who lived here?

"Its Damian and Tanya's."

"It looks like they've been here for a while."

"A few years."

While they were talking he let his eyes peruse the room, taking in one odd object after another until he noticed a photograph framed in a round peace symbol. It was two colorfully dressed young people looking like they were totally infatuated with each other.

"Is that them?" pointing to the photo.

"In their hippie days."

"So this is what happens to aging hippies, at least in Bolinas."

"In this particular case, yes."

"It looks like they've been here since the 60's."

"That we have." Damian had overheard the conversation and decided to fill in the answer. The father and kids put their attention on him, waiting to see if he would elaborate. Finally, the father ventured forth, "Your home looks like the accumulation of a life well-lived."

"Well, that's a very good way of putting it," Damian said, "and we," saying the 'we' loud enough for Tanya, who was in the kitchen, to hear, "we hope to continue." He gave her a smile that accentuated the wrinkles lining his face, just as the cobwebs had grown around the photograph on the top shelf between an old piece of driftwood and a God's eye.

I noticed some faded writing on the wall by the boulders, by the beach entrance, something about *an angel*. Did someone die there?"

Damian was momentarily taken back by the question. His demeanor changed, from a joyful host to a thoughtful one. He was there but the father could see an absence in his eyes.

"Yes," he finally said in a soft tone, someone did die there."

Not wanting to pry but wanting to acknowledge what he sensed, the father said, "It looks like it's still a traumatic memory."

"Yes, I guess I haven't thought about her for a long time."

"It was a woman?"

"A young woman, about sixteen, she was just sixteen..."

Hesitating, yet wanting to know, he ventured to ask him, "What happened to her?"

"Well..." he pulled up a chair and sat down, "Do you really want to know?"

"I don't mean to pry, but it sounds like one of the mysteries of this town."

"Well, we do have mysteries here, but she was not a mystery, she was an unfortunate victim of an accident, of circumstances, of a very strange summer,"

"What summer?"

"It was 1966, the year before the so-called *summer of love* but in Bolinas we, at least, Tanya and I, called it the *summer of tragedy and ecstasy...*"

"Yes, she was young and innocent and we were all caught up in whatever was happening until something happened that none of us anticipated or wanted."

"She died?"

"Yes, she died, and I'm going to have to leave it at that. Maybe someone else can fill you in if you're interested but, as you can see, we've made a home here and learned to live with that past..."

He left them and let them finish their meal. The couple at their table had also been listening and ventured to add something to the conversation, "That's not the only story to come out of Bolinas," the man said.

"What do you mean?"

"Well, there is the on-going enigma of the woman who disappeared."

"Disappeared," the oldest boy questioned.

"Yup, you can still hear her moaning in the winds going through the Eucalyptus trees."

Their ears perked up when he said something about a moaning sound."

"I think we heard her," the youngest child said, his eyes growing larger.

"There was a man who came into Bolinas that summer looking for his wife. He said she had disappeared, and one evening, while asking about her, he saw her scarf on the beach, on this giant metal sculpture that a local beachcomber had built."

"And, did he find her?"

"Well, to make a long story short, he kept looking for her, along the coast..."

"Did he ever find her?"

"You know, I don't think so, but I'm not absolutely sure. We saw him on several occasions. He kept coming back to Bolinas every summer for years...staying with Mariah, who used to run a café called Scowleys across the street from Smileys..." The kids snickered at the ironic playfulness of the names. "Sometimes I saw him walking along the beach, listening...Sometimes he stayed with this beachcomber called Hollywood who used to live on the beach..."

"We saw some people camped on the beach today," the youngest child said."

"Yea, well, there's always someone out there, it's one of the last places some people can call home..."

After they had eaten and told Damian they would keep the mystery eatery a mystery, they said good-bye and walked back to the Grandiose. Their day had been long and the night was welcomed. In the morning they decided to leave after breakfast, hoping to visit the bird sanctuary, or explore another beach at the western end of the mesa. As they started driving along Mesa Road the father started singing a few words, *good byyyye Bolinas we'll see you again*...the kids picked up the melody and added some more words, *good byyyye Bolinas we don't know just when,*
Good byyyye Bolinas let's trip into thennnnnn boop boop boop dee do do do dee boop boop boop dee do do do
We've played on your beach and we've rolled down your sand
We've seen your lagoon and we've played with your band
Your salmon was a welcome hit and your morning sweet roll nearly gave us a fit
Good byyyye Bolinas wherever you are
Good byyye Bolinas you're never too far
Good byyye Bolinas let's trip the bizarre
boop boop boop dee do do do dee boop boop boop dee do do do...

45

Life's Endings

Life's endings are death, at least biological death, the life force ebbs out and a man or a woman turns cold while we hold their hand, slowly the hand turns cold and the face turns gray grayer as the blood ends it's coursing. Most novels end as stories end with some closure whether ending a way of life or embarking on a new journey...Life's endings are not cozy, in fact they may go on for years in inner agony, in solitary confinement, in solitude, in sickness, in quiet desperation, in subdued, oppressed acceptance.

I watched him sitting in the darkened corner of the L.O.V.E. café in Amsterdam, this balding longhaired lean faced man. When he looked up I could feel his presence, although his eyes were barely open. He was smoking a joint with the smoke occasionally obscuring his face. I thought I had seen him in Dam Square singing left over folk songs. He had papers in front of him, abstractly colored flyers that he had written on – *awake to ecstatic moments – live in the present – be here now*...out of some age-old urging, I got up and decided to engage him. What was there to lose?

"I heard you singing yesterday."
Only his eyes moved.
"There was one song that I could live in."
"Yea."
"Yea, the one about crazy ideals."
He smiled.
"I liked it. It really reminded me of a time I thought I had left behind, when I was a bit younger or let me put it this way it reminded of the years after the 60's, after I left the madness…I guess I grew out of it…"
"I guess so."
"So, why'd you write that, as a reminiscence of that time? Did you lose something?"
The man looked at him, no one, that he could remember, had asked him that simple question. He shrugged and chuckled to himself.
"Yea, I've lost something."
"Well, you made up for it with that song."
"I wouldn't know about that, but the song came out one night, one dream night that took me back. It was one of those that pretty much wrote it self."
"Do you have the lyrics?"
Before a word was spoken in response, his eyes shut, time slowed until he started to talk and sing…
Disillusioned and disheartened
Well, you think the world has forgotten
What you tried to do
When you wore your heart
For all to see, hey hey hey
for all to see
Your crazy ideals, what have they brought you?
Your crazy ideals, where have they got you?
Your crazy ideals, just look around
And you will see
He took a breath, sighed and started to talk, to recite,
A tree takes time to grow
And mountains may just know
How long it takes
To be what we imagine
How long it takes for us to see
For us to see
That what is done is not in vain
His voice wavered. I could see an eye glistening through the smoke,
Every act and every gain has worth now
Your daughters have more choices now
And people have gained voices now
That were still
Demonstrations have made their point
And children take for granted what's been done

What's been one
Step at a time
Step at a time
The café had turned silent, his voice rolled through the air, the words oozed out, penetrating the walls and every one who listened to this paean to the 60s social crusaders and their ideals to intrude on their intimate public lives.
Some people are in the news
And they bring on their views of tyranny
Through subtle influence
And armed incidents
By now his voice had taken on gravel mixed with emotion. There was no stopping him now,
Something they couldn't stand
Something they fought against
Oh no no no no
Your crazy ideals
What did they leave you
Your crazy ideals
Where did they lead you
Your crazy ideals
Just look around and you will see
Well, a tree takes time to grow
And rivers may just know how long it takes to be
What we imagine
How long it takes
For us to see
For us to see
That freedoms's not a constant thing
And each of us must try to bring it back again
And every gain may fade away
Like waves that take the shore away
To remind us
That stylish masks may hide the soul
But the devil who is taking toll's
Behind us
And will ride us
Yes will ride ride ride
Now glory is a constant thing
And if it's real it's got to ring in ourselves
In what we choose to do
In what is right to do
That only we can do
Come on come on
It's up to you
And your crazy ideals
They may just be true

Your crazy ideals
They may just be you
Your crazy ideals
Just look inside
And you will see
You will see
Your crazy ideals…

The room, the haze, the habitués had changed…I had changed, he had resurrected a past that was could have been…We let the last ideal soak into the walls, the floor boards, the leftover reminders living in us. After the last ideal quieted down, I asked him,

"You still believe that?"

"Time can make a fool of us, yet we still go on. Ultimately we live out our lives with the memories of what we have quote: 'tried to do' unquote.

"Is it a strong belief that keeps us going? Even if we are wrong or not sure?"

"The lessons of history might teach us something. If you think, for example, that the relative freedom of an individual is important, then you might consider the times and places that spawned that idea and actually tried to put it in place; the agora of Athens, where freedom and responsibility were debated; the palace of Babylon, where Hammerabi codified rules or laws to live by; the tree under which Gautama sat and realized freedom is letting go of desire or in Monticello, where Jefferson urged other community leaders and landowners to separate religion from the governing of the community and make religion an inner relationship with your spiritual belief. Can you imagine he was considered the voice of the devil by some of the ministers of that time. Sounds familiar, doesn't it? For over 200 years the dominant culture in North America has struggled with the issues of freedom and responsibility and the separation of powers that govern our larger nation state, our communities and ultimately ourselves."

"I wasn't expecting a lecture from him but his words still held me."

"Right from the beginning these framers of the governing scaffold recognized that minority rights, that individual rights had to be protected. Imagine these ideas and the attempts to implement them at a time when most of the world's cultures were traditional, patriarchical, monarchical or despotic. It seems every major culture had developed it's social hierarchies, ours included, with it's slaves and indentured servants on the one hand to the god-sanctioned rulers on the other…these framers, while working out of the destruction of the Indian cultures on this continent, which is not an easy history to justify, mind you, still inspired and instigated, even more, lived out ideas that they considered deeply and with gratefulness. Out of that bloody soil came ideas and ways of governing that have given promise to millions of people in the world. Slavery was one of the great issues and a tremendous struggle for the founding fathers and the nation. Ideas take time to grow because they came out of the fields of human needs and long time survival patterns of the strongest families, clans, groups and eventually organized power states. Throughout this history people carried out heinous crimes and cruel acts punctuated with moments of joy and love and inspired rules of social behavior…

I just nodded my head in recognition of his thoughts until he abruptly changed his tone and asked,

"Now why," he said, almost as an afterthought, "are you so interested in my song?"

The man thought for a moment turned back to him and raised his palm. In the middle of it the smoke-filled singer could see the vague outline of an old scar.

"Peace," he spoke quietly and walked out of the L.O.V.E. café…

46

Epiphany

So, is that it, is that the end? Aren't you going to ask how Sweet knew about this meeting in Amsterdam? How does she know about this meeting; these thoughts? Well, you supply the answers. You go to Vermont and tell her you've seen Shiva, lost in smoke, in Amsterdam. Show her your scar, your scar of youth, your scar of lost ecstasy, your once upon a lifetime plunge into that which is too soon gone, which is the world's loss and maybe just cannot exist for too long a time any time. The closest we have is an orgasm that can stop time. Remember that the world came close to this explosion, had come close…

And Bolinas was in the midst of it in the throes of it in the throbbing, shaking wavering wanting needing crazy woozy bluesy blows of it…

And Bolinas was in the midst of the everlasting momentary epiphany of it…

Goodbyyye Bolinas…
We'll see you again…
Good byyye Bolinas
We don't know just when…

211

Postlude

The room had gotten cooler but no one had noticed. Time had slowed. A lifetime had gone by. Forrest had drifted off in his wicker chair, surrounded by blankets, the two older boys had tried to hold on until they could see Bolinas again…Ellyn was resting her eyes in a contemplative finalitude.

"So I was right, you never did find her?" Barbara promulgated, "She is still lost, a metaphoric unknown, somewhere on or off the coast of California…"

With that, Bob woke up and added the *amen*, "Maybe she just slid off the continent, became one of the illusions we cling too, stranger things have happened…"

The On-going

Acknowledgements

Everyone's youth is extraordinary, an awakening to the world. I feel privileged to have been born in a time of monumental change. My teenage years were a complex mixture of western United States history, church community and the increasing inroads of bicoastal ferment. I was a junior in high school when the tragic pall of John Kennedy's death fell into our hallways. We were not immune to world changing events but my life revolved around church softball games, deer hunting, washing my '56' Chevy, listening to the top ten, and the thrill of first love.

I visited San Francisco in 1965 and 1967 being forever touched by the incredible social upheaval. I vowed that I would one day return. After many wonderful and sometimes emotionally difficult years I ended up looking out on the Pacific. Bolinas became a part of my many sojourns along the coast.

It is a mythical Bolinas that is found in the pages of this book yet it also reverberates with my upbringing before Utah. This connection is to a much older culture and home land and the great human tragedy of the 20th Century. Out of that came great empathy for suffering and, just as important, appreciation for the life-affirming moments of joy.

It is in this spirit, with coffee in hand, that I think about the many people who have been a part of my life, letting them surround me and walk with me again…Thank you.

Other words

Masama – a novella of twin brothers finding each other. Published by Xlibris.com

Labyrinth   a mythic journey – a novel of two brothers finding themselves while on a timeless journey – from the days of yore to the techno halls of innovation.

Published by ebookstand.com

On the Wings of a Swan - an allegory of love transcending the everyday - with watercolor illustrations by the author.

Available through highwayone.net

from Pigeon Point to Point Reyes – a book of pastels and haikus of the California coast.

Available through Lulu.com

I Am Always With You! by Marianne Neumann – my mother's journal from 1938 to 1945. Translated by the author. A beautiful love story in the midst of war.

Available through highwayone.net